Large Print Chi
Child, Maureen.
The last Santini virgin

STACKS

WITHDRAWN

# The Last Santini Virgin

**MAUREEN CHILD**

*All the characters in this book have no existence outside the imagination of the author, and have no relation whatsoever to anyone bearing the same name or names. They are not even distantly inspired by any individual known or unknown to the author, and all the incidents are pure invention.*

*All Rights Reserved including the right of reproduction in whole or in part in any form. This edition is published by arrangement with Harlequin Enterprises II B.V. The text of this publication or any part thereof may not be reproduced or transmitted in any form or by any means, electronic or mechanical, including photocopying, recording, storage in an information retrieval system, or otherwise, without the written permission of the publisher.*

*Silhouette, Silhouette Desire and Colophon are registered trademarks of Harlequin Books S.A., used under licence.*

*First published in Great Britain 2001*
*Large Print edition 2004*
*Silhouette Books Limited,*
*Eton House, 18-24 Paradise Road,*
*Richmond, Surrey TW9 1SR*

© Maureen Child 2000

ISBN 0 373 04923 4

*Set in Times Roman 18½ on 20 pt.*
*36-0704-39848*

*Printed and bound in Great Britain*
*by Antony Rowe Ltd, Chippenham, Wiltshire*

***MAUREEN CHILD***

was born and raised in Southern California and is the only person she knows who longs for an occasional change of season. She is delighted to be writing for Silhouette® and is especially excited to be a part of the Desire™ line.

An avid reader, Maureen looks forward to those rare rainy California days when she can curl up and sink into a good book. Or two. When she isn't busy writing, she and her husband of twenty-five years like to travel, leaving their two grown-up children in charge of the neurotic golden retriever who is the *real* head of the household. Maureen is also an award-winning historical writer under the names Kathleen Kane and Ann Carberry.

NEWARK PUBLIC LIBRARY
NEWARK, OHIO 43055-5054

Large Print Chi
Child, Maureen.
The last Santini virgin

8040512

For my cousin,
Kathy Carberry Makowski,
who, like the rest of us, may get
knocked down, but always gets up.

# One

"Move that hand, Marine," Gina Santini said firmly, "or lose it."

Gunnery Sergeant Nick Paretti chuckled and slowly, deliberately, slid his hand higher up her back, away from her behind. "What's the matter, princess?" he asked. "Do I make you nervous?"

*Nervous* didn't quite cover it, she thought. For three and a half weeks, now, she'd been spending three nights a week in this man's arms. And it wasn't getting any easier.

Although she was annoyed by Nick's arrogance, the real problem was her attraction to him. It was no use trying to argue with her own hormones. But for Heaven's sake, how could she feel such electricity for a man who'd made it his life's work to irritate her?

"You're trying to lead again." His deep voice shook her, as always, and she resented him for that, too.

Gina tilted her head way back and looked up into her dance partner's eyes. "Maybe I wouldn't have to lead if you'd remember the steps."

"And maybe," Nick nearly growled, "I'd remember the steps if you wouldn't quit changing the rhythm on me."

She inhaled deeply and counted to ten. Then twenty. Nope, she was still mad. She tried to drag her right hand free of the man's iron grip, but it was like trying to pull a train with a compact car. Ballroom dance lessons had seemed like such a good idea a month ago. But how could she have known that she'd be paired with a man too tall, too broad and too stubborn?

"Look, General," she said.

"Gunnery Sergeant," he corrected her. "Or Nick."

Apparently, he was feeling magnanimous tonight.

"Nick," she said, trying to sound cooperative, "we're both paying a lot of money for these lessons. Don't you think we should be working together to get the most out of them?"

"I'm doing my share, honey," he told her, his blue eyes staring steadily into hers. "Our problems start when *you* try to do my share, too."

Okay, so she had a little problem with leading and following. But that was better than letting him indulge his tendency to stomp her toes into oblivion.

"Fine," she said. "You lead. Only this time try not to crush my toes."

One black eyebrow lifted. "If you didn't have such big feet, they wouldn't be in the way."

Gina stiffened. She was just a little sensitive about the size of her feet. Was it her fault that her mother's size-four feet had not been handed down to her? "Believe it or not," she said tightly, "no one else in the world has trouble avoiding my toes."

"Luck," he muttered.

"And don't call me honey," she snapped.

Gina's gaze drifted around the room. Five other couples seemed to be gliding effortlessly across the highly polished wood floor. No one else appeared to be battling constantly with their partner.

"Do we have to argue our way through every lesson?" she whispered more to herself than to him.

"No argument here, princess," Nick said, bending his head toward hers and keeping his voice low, "as long as you admit that I'm the man and I'm supposed to lead."

Was he going to grunt and pound his chest next?

"So," he asked as the music swelled around them, "you ready now?"

"As I'll ever be," she said.

"Let's get it done, then." He paused, and she watched him listening to the music, catching the beat. Then he took a deep breath and threw them both into the deep end of the dancing pool. As they executed their first turn, he gave her a fleeting half smile.

Lucky for her it was gone so fast, she thought as she silently acknowledged the thud of her heartbeat. Those occasional smiles of his were nerve-racking. No other man had ever affected her like this. And Gina wasn't at all sure she liked it. On the other hand, there didn't seem to be much she could do about it.

The moment they'd been assigned to each other as partners, there'd been fireworks. Not the nice, safe, pretty ones you saw at choreographed Fourth of July shows. Nope, these were down-and-dirty, completely illegal, bottle-rocket fireworks. Hot flashes, brilliant light and a breathtaking sense of imminent danger.

Gina gulped in a breath, pushed that thought right out of her head and concentrated on the present situation. The overhead fluorescent lights seemed to blur slightly as they danced. On the hardwood floor, the colorful shadows of the moving couples swayed and dipped as if there were another world beneath the floor and

Gina and Nick, as well as all the others, were the actual reflections.

"You know, we're getting pretty good at this," he murmured, and his voice rumbled along her spine.

"Don't get cocky," she warned just before they stumbled slightly.

He scowled at her. "A little positive thinking wouldn't be out of line, here."

A little rhythm wouldn't hurt, either, she thought, but didn't say. Why was he doing this? she wondered for probably the hundredth time since being assigned Nick Paretti as a dance partner. She had a perfectly good reason for being there, of course. She loved dancing. At least she had until recently.

But *he* was a mystery. A big, burly Marine, from his military-cut, black hair to the spit shine on his exceptionally heavy shoes, he just didn't seem the type to sign up for dance class. Hand grenades, yes. Waltzes, no.

Plus, he was way too good-looking for comfort. Black hair, piercing blue eyes, square jaw; a nose that looked as though it had been smacked once or twice—she could understand why—and a mouth that could curve into a mocking smile that practically curled her toes.

Oh, my.

The music ended, and Gina stepped back out of his arms. Instantly she felt the loss of him and told herself it meant nothing. She was simply used to the feel of him pressed against her.

"That went well, I think," their teacher, Mrs. Stanton, called from her spot at the edge of the dance floor. The woman's bright-blond hair was swept back into a tight knot at the top of her head, and as she walked into the crowd of dancers, her full skirt swished and swirled around her knees. "Most of you seem to be progressing nicely," she added, then shot Nick a look that was pure female admiration, and Gina wanted to kick something. "But, ladies, you must remember to trust your partner. The dance floor is not the place for a battle of the sexes."

"Hmm," Nick wondered aloud. "You suppose she meant that one for you?"

"Don't you have to invade a country somewhere?" Gina asked sweetly.

He laughed and shook his head.

"Now, class," Mrs. Stanton said as she walked back toward the small stereo set up in the corner, "the cha-cha."

"Oh, man..." Nick's disgusted groan was just the thing to cheer Gina up.

"What's the matter, General? Scared?" she asked.

"Sergeant. Gunnery Sergeant, as a matter of fact." He gave her a glare.

"I've mentioned it a time or two already."

She shrugged. "Like it matters."

"Lady," he said, inhaling deeply enough to swell his already broad chest to massive proportions. "You are—"

"Better at the cha-cha than you?" she said, interrupting him.

He gave her a fierce scowl. "That'll be the day."

"Why, General," Gina said with a grin, "I do believe that's a challenge."

"Take it any way you want," he said, and reached out to grab her.

"Oh, very smooth," Gina taunted as he pulled her closely against him.

"You know," he said thoughtfully as he stared down into her eyes, "you're the reason there *is* a battle of the sexes."

Gina put her left hand on his shoulder and slipped her right hand into his left.

"Right. Gina Santini is the mother of all problems between the sexes."

"Not you personally," he continued, and held her right hand a little tighter than necessary. "Women like you."

"Ah," she said with a nod and a teasing smile, "women who don't swoon at you warrior types?"

He took a deep breath, blew it out again and asked, "Are we going to dance or what?"

She batted her eyelashes at him and said, "I'm waiting for you. You're the fearless leader, remember?"

Grumbling under his breath, Nick started moving to the rhythm of the music. Gina concentrated on following his lead rather than trying to plot their course around the floor. She knew he hated the cha-cha, but she loved it. There was something about the way he held her for this dance. The way their hips moved against each other.

Uh-oh. Better not go there.

They executed a turn, and she silently admitted that her generation was missing a lot with all of the wild, contortionist dances that were so popular now. There was so much more to be said for the closeness of ballroom dancing.

Too much, really, she thought as she felt Nick's pelvis move against her. Fires stirred within and she closed her eyes briefly. When she opened them again, she met his gaze and saw flickers of heat shifting in his eyes. One of his hands dropped to the curve of her behind, and Gina would have sworn she felt the brand of each of his fingertips.

"Much better, Sergeant and Gina," Mrs. Stanton called out as they cha-cha'd past her.

Gina automatically stiffened her spine and lifted her chin.

"Teacher's pet," Nick mumbled with a brief smile.

"Delinquent," she muttered.

"How'd you guess?"

"What?"

"That I was a delinquent when I was a kid."

Was he serious? He practically had Bad Boy stenciled on his forehead. "I'm psychic."

"Too bad you're not a tall psychic," he said.

Five foot five wasn't exactly an amazon, but she didn't qualify for kids' ticket prices at the movies, either. "I'm not short," she told him. "You're abnormally tall."

"I'm only six-four, which is hardly Godzilla."

"Depends on your point of view."

He blew out an exasperated sigh. "I wasn't trying to start World War III," he complained. "I'm just saying I'm getting a crick in my neck looking down at you."

"Well looking up all night isn't a picnic, ya know."

Ridiculous to argue over nothing, but it was certainly safer than concentrating on how he was making her feel. Their hips moved against each other again, and Gina flushed, her body awakening to the closeness of Nick's.

Was dancing supposed to be this sexy? Nick wondered as he pressed Gina even closer to him, hoping as he did so that she couldn't feel the arousal tightening the fit of his slacks. She felt so small, so defenseless in his arms. Yet even as that thought entered his mind, he wanted to chuckle. Gina? Defenseless? Yeah, like a hungry tiger.

This tiny woman was able to give as good as she got, and he'd found himself almost looking forward to their three-times-a-week shoot-outs. She had a smart-alecky, completely kissable mouth, a compact body that curved in all the right places and a head harder than his.

All in all, just the kind of woman he'd be interested in if he was looking for a woman, which he wasn't. Now he supposed most men wouldn't be captivated by a woman who argued anything at the drop of a stick. But Nick had been raised in a good old-fashioned Italian family, where love was measured in octaves reached while yelling.

His mother had told him once that arguments were the spice of married life. And if she'd been telling the truth, then his folks had had one spicy marriage for the past thirty-six years. He smiled to himself as memories crowded into his brain. His two brothers, his parents and himself, seated at the dinner table, arguing about politics, religion, history or even, on a slow day, who was stronger, Superman or Mighty Mouse. The Paretti house was loud, but it was happy.

The cha-cha ended, and the couples on the floor slowly stopped, turning toward Mrs. Stanton, awaiting instructions. Nick dropped Gina's hand, then curled his own fingers into a fist so he didn't notice how empty his hand felt without hers in it.

"That's all for tonight, everyone," the teacher said.

He ignored the shaft of disappointment that sliced through him. Two hours passed mighty damn quickly in this place.

"But I want you all to think about something," she went on. "The Bayside Amateur Dance Competition is next month, and we've been invited to enter three couples from our class."

A ripple of conversation rose up and then faded as Mrs. Stanton continued. "Next week I'll be selecting the three couples who will represent my little dance school, so do your very best, and good luck to you all."

He caught the excited gleam in Gina's eyes.

A competition?

In *public?* Oh, he didn't think so.

# Two

**O**nce class ended, Nick walked outside, barely listening to Gina's stream of chatter. He kept envisioning himself dancing in public. And those mental pictures were enough to give him chills.

Hell, the whole reason he was taking these classes was because of what had happened the last time he'd danced in public. It was at last year's Marine Corps Ball. In front of everyone. In a flash he remembered it all.

A crowded room, hundreds of people and him, dancing with a major's wife. Or rather, *trying* to dance. She'd cajoled him into it, and he'd reluctantly given in. But as the dance had gone on, he'd almost relaxed…until the moment he'd spun her. Somehow she'd slipped free, and he'd watched, helplessly, as she'd sailed directly into the punch bowl.

Nick swallowed a groan at the memory and quickly pushed the rest of it aside. He really didn't want to remember the crash of the punch bowl, the splash of liquid, the major's wife's screech or the image of the poor woman sitting on the dance floor drenched in ruby-red punch.

Instead he clearly recalled the meeting he'd had a week later with the major.

"You cost me about $250, Gunny," the officer had said. "It seems even a talented dry cleaner can't get red punch out of ivory silk."

Standing at ease, but certainly not feeling it, Nick offered, "I'd be happy to pay to replace the dress, sir."

"Not necessary," the Major told him as he stood up from behind his desk and walked around to stop just inches from him. "But I suggest you make sure this never happens again."

"It won't, sir," Nick assured him. "I'll avoid the dance floor at all costs."

"That's not what I meant."

"Sir?"

The Major perched on the edge of his desk, crossed his arms over his chest and shook his head. "You know as well as I do that 'attendance is expected, and body movement at these things will be noticed.'"

Nick winced internally. The Corps couldn't *order* a man to show up and dance, but they managed to get the point across, anyway.

"So before you toss some other poor woman into a punch bowl, I *suggest,* Gunnery Sergeant," the man said in a low growl, "that you learn what to do on a dance floor."

Panic, clean and sharp, whistled through him as he realized what the officer was telling him to do. "You can't be serious, sir. *Dance* lessons?"

The other man stared at him for a long minute before asking, "Do I look like I'm kidding?"

Nick groaned tightly at the memory before tucking it into a dark corner of his mind. Hell. He had to be the first Marine in history to have been ordered into a dance class. Well, technically not "ordered." He'd been "suggested" into it. He would much rather the Major had sentenced him to a few thirty-mile hikes. Or had him transferred to Greenland.

But, no. That would have been too easy a punishment.

Instead Nick was stuck practicing to be a second-rate Fred Astaire. And, oh, man, what his friends would say if they knew what he was up to. For weeks after the punch bowl incident, he'd put up with the teasing, the jokes, the near-constant barrage of abuse from his friends. Hell, if they ever found out that he was actually taking ballroom dance lessons, they'd never let him forget it. As for dancing in a *contest?* He'd probably have to resign from the Corps just to get some peace.

Nope. What he had to do was survive this stupid class then get back to being a full-time Marine.

Of course, when the classes were over, he wouldn't be seeing Gina again. Surprising really, how much that realization bothered him.

A cold, damp breeze slinked in off the

ocean and swept the rest of old memories and troubling thoughts from his mind. He returned his attention just in time to the short woman walking—or rather, *running* along beside him.

"Are you listening to me?" she asked, and judging from the exasperation in her tone, it wasn't for the first time.

Nick stopped, looked down at her and shook his head. "If you're still talking about that competition, no."

She threw her hands wide and let them fall to her sides again. "Why not?"

That mouth of hers looked good even in a frown. Oh, no, he wasn't going there. Leaving his hormones out of the equation, Gina Santini was not going to get to him. "A better question, princess, is why are you so hot to enter a contest with me when all you can do is complain about how badly I dance?"

The wind tossed her dark-brown curls

around her face, and Gina reached up with one hand to push them back from her eyes. "You're really not totally bad."

Heartwarming. "Gee," he said, sarcasm dripping from his words, "thanks."

She pulled in a deep breath, which distracted him momentarily by drawing his gaze to the curve of her breasts, then she sighed dramatically. "It's a contest," she said as if that was enough to explain everything. "Don't you want to win?"

That gleam in her eyes was back again, and a part of Nick admired her. He liked a good competition, too. He just preferred entering contests that he had some small chance of winning.

"We're not good enough," he said flatly, and started for his car again, hoping she'd drop the subject.

He should have known better.

Right behind him, he heard the heels of her shoes tapping against the asphalt as she trotted to keep up with his long-legged stride.

"We could be," she said, "good enough, I mean."

Nick laughed shortly.

"All we'd need is extra practice."

"Yeah," he agreed, "for a year or two."

"For Pete's sake, General," Gina said, and stepped in front of him, bringing him to a quick stop. "Do all Marines give up as easily as you?"

A quick flash of irritation swelled up inside him.

"Marines do not give up, princess," he said, and loomed over her, which wasn't hard since she was so darn short. "We simply choose our battles."

"Uh-huh. Apparently only the ones you're sure of winning."

"Look," he said, and threw his car a longing glance before looking at Gina again. Obviously, he wasn't going to get out of here without yet another argument. And to think that only a moment ago he'd been bothered by the thought of never seeing her again. God. What had he done in his life to deserve this irritating, too-damned-attractive woman? Answer: he'd thrown a major's wife into a punch bowl.

"You said yourself all we do is argue. Do you really want to spend *more* time together?"

She folded her arms under her breasts and he absolutely refused to look. It wasn't easy, but he kept his gaze locked with hers. One of her finely arched eyebrows went just a bit higher. "We wouldn't argue so much if you weren't so stubborn."

"Hah! *I'm* stubborn?"

She gave him a look that would have fried a lesser man's soul. Then, clearly disgusted, she asked, "Why am I even talking to you?"

"You got me, princess."

"Will you *stop* calling me princess?"

"As soon as you stop acting like one."

Her big brown eyes widened and then narrowed dangerously. "What's that supposed to mean?"

Well, hell. He hadn't really meant to say that out loud. "Never mind."

"Oh, no, you don't," she said. "Explain."

"There's no reason to go into any of this," he hedged. He didn't want to hurt her feelings. He just didn't want to enter that blasted contest. "It's late. I've got to get back to base."

She leaned back against his car and shook her head. For such a tiny woman, she had the look of an immovable object.

"You started this, Sergeant. Now you finish it."

This was his own fault, he told himself. He never should have said what he was thinking. But Gina had a way of irking him like no one else he'd ever known.

He swept his gaze up and down her compact, curvy form before coming to rest on those beautiful brown eyes of hers. And damned if she didn't know just how pretty she was, too. Oh, not that she seemed conceited, but there was a confidence about her that came from knowing she presented a hell of a picture. And the more he thought about it, the more he realized how right he was in his assessment of her. Pampered, spoiled, obviously used to getting her own way, she was completely unprepared for someone—*anyone* saying no to her.

"So, General," she said, "do you explain, or do we stand here all night?"

All around them their fellow students were leaving the tiny parking lot. Overhead, dark clouds sailed across a black sky, obliterating the stars and threatening rain. Even in southern California, January weather could be unpredictable. And just in case it was going to start raining anytime soon, he decided to end this debate once and for all. If she wanted the truth that badly, she could have it.

"It means that I know you better than you think I do."

"Oh, really?"

It didn't take a rocket scientist, he told himself. She was Italian. So was he. And if there was one thing he knew, it was Italian families.

"Youngest in your family, weren't you?"

She flinched slightly. "So?"

"The apple of daddy's eye?"

She straightened up away from the car. Squaring her shoulders, she lifted her chin, glared at him and asked, "Your point?"

Ah…direct hit.

"My point is that you've spent your entire life getting exactly what you want just by batting those gorgeous eyes of yours." He leaned in closer and knew instantly it had been a mistake. Her perfume distracted him, but he steeled himself against that potent scent and finished what he had to say. "Well, it's not gonna work with me, princess. We're partners on that dance floor, because we're stuck with each other. But you can save that wide-eyed, innocent look for the college boys, all right?"

It took her a minute to calm down enough to talk.

Then she started sputtering. "You are the single most irritating, annoying, overbearing, insulting—" She paused and bit her bottom lip.

A bottom lip he suddenly wanted to kiss more than he wanted to draw his next breath. The other couples were driving away, and the flash of headlights skimmed across her face and faded again, leaving only the dim glow of the yellow fog lights in the parking lot. Streamers of gray, damp fog drifted in from the ocean and twined around their legs, linking them together in an otherworldly grip.

Seconds passed, ticking by as they stared at each other. She was so close. Close enough to kiss. To touch. He lifted one hand, and as she leaned in toward him a car horn sounded, shattering the weird spell that had been cast over them.

She shook her head as if coming up out of a dream. "I, uh, have to go."

"Yeah. Me, too."

She opened her mouth to say something more, but snapped it shut again a moment later. Then, without giving him another look, she turned around and marched off across the shadowy parking lot toward her car.

Nick watched her go and told himself he was only keeping an eye on her to see that she made it into her car safely. After all, a pretty woman, a deserted parking lot, it was the decent thing to do. But he was still standing there, staring after her, long after she'd pulled out of the lot and driven off.

The next day after work, Nick entered the Staff NCO club and headed down the wide hallway. Absently he took the short flight of steps, passed the small reception area and climbed five more steps to the darkened ballroom. As he stepped into the familiar club, he turned to his right and stopped just at the long mahogany bar. His gaze swept the shadow-filled room. A huge place, it looked nearly empty, with just a sprinkling of tables dotting the floor. But when the room was decked out for a ball or a party, the old club shone like a gem.

The few noncommissioned officers seated at the tables barely glanced his way. He recognized a few familiar faces in the bunch. But on a base the size of Pendleton, it wasn't unusual to see a lot of strangers as well as friends.

He leaned his elbows on the bar, ordered a beer and, as he had been doing all day, relived those last few minutes in the dark with Gina. Gritting his teeth, he told himself for the thousandth time that he'd had no right to stomp on her feelings like that. So what if she irritated him? That didn't give him leave to fire mortar rounds at her heart.

And, damn it, he was sure he'd seen her eyes go all teary.

Great, he thought as the bartender slid

his beer in front of him. Big, strong Marine had made a woman cry.

He took a long swallow of beer and tried to rinse the taste of disgust from his mouth as another Marine entered the bar and walked up beside him. "Paretti?"

Half turning, he looked at the man, noted the insignia on his shirtsleeve and recognized him as another Gunnery Sergeant. "Yeah?"

The guy stuck out his right hand and said, "Thought it was you. I'm Davis Garvey."

"I've seen you around," Nick said with a nod as he shook the man's hand, then turned to pay the bartender for his beer. Glancing back at Davis, he asked, "You want anything?"

"No, thanks," he said, and waved the bartender off. "I'm on my way home. Just stopped in to look for you, actually."

"Now why would you do that?" Nick

asked, and took another sip of his drink, wishing the guy would leave so he could get on with torturing himself for picking on Gina.

The other man grinned and leaned one elbow on the bar. "Sort of promised my new sister-in-law I would."

Nick looked at the guy, trying to figure out what was going on here. As far as he knew, he hadn't dated any women lately who had brothers-in-law stationed at Pendleton. So it couldn't be some defending-her-honor kind of thing. And if this was leading to a "shotgun wedding" scenario, the man would just have to go ahead and shoot him. No way was Nick Paretti getting married again. The phrase "been there, done that" roared across his mind.

"Okay," he said after a minute or two of silence, "you have my attention. What's up?"

Around them conversations flowed, Marines relaxed after a long hard day, and splashes of laughter shot through the air. But Nick wasn't paying attention to any of it. Instead, he concentrated on the man now grinning like some damned fool.

"I hear," Davis said, "you've been making Gina's life miserable at dancing school."

Panic, swift and sure, shot through him.

"Hey!" Nick spoke up quickly, then threw a fast glance at the Marines on either side of them to make sure they hadn't been listening in. After all the trouble he'd been going to, to keep his dancing lessons a secret, he sure wasn't about to stand there and let Davis Garvey announce it in the NCO club. Hell, the news would be all over base by morning.

He could almost hear the teasing and

ribbing he'd be getting for the rest of his life if word got out. They would be calling him Sergeant Twinkle-Toes or something else just as humiliating. For Pete's sake, he had to get Garvey out of there.

Wouldn't you just know Gina would be involved in this? All of his guilty feelings melted away to be replaced by the irritation he usually felt for the woman.

"Why don't we go outside to talk about this?" he suggested, and took a huge swallow of beer when he'd finished talking.

Davis's grin broadened, and his eyes held a knowing gleam. Yep, he knew exactly why Nick was trying to get him to leave the club. "Oh, I don't know. I'm happy right here."

Scowling at his fellow sergeant, Nick muttered, "Look, I'm not going to talk about it in here, all right?"

Then he turned around, marched out of

the room and down the first flight of stairs like a man on the parade ground. He never looked back, never checked to be sure Garvey was following him. Just kept walking, across the reception area, up the short flight of steps and out the doors into the late-afternoon gloom. Nick kept walking until he reached his car, and there he stopped, waiting.

In another minute or two Davis Garvey approached slowly, hands in his pockets, that damned smirk still on his face.

"All right, what's this about?" Nick snapped.

"I told you. Gina."

Figured. It wasn't enough that she drove him crazy at class. Now she'd thought of a way to bother him at work, too. And to think he'd spent all day berating himself for hurting her feelings. "She's your sister-in-law, you said?"

"Yep. I married her sister Marie a couple of weeks ago."

"Congratulations," Nick muttered, and silently wished the poor guy luck. He'd need it if his new wife was anything like her sister.

"Thanks."

He didn't want to insult the man's family, but damned if Nick was going to stand there and not defend himself, either. "Since you're related to her, you should know what Gina's like."

"Charming?" Davis suggested. "Beautiful? Funny?"

All of the above, Nick thought, and plenty more. "Don't forget to add annoying, shrewish, bossy..." He paused, then asked, "Do I have to go on?"

"No," Davis said on a laugh. Shaking his head slightly, he added, "I think I get the picture."

"I'm not sure you do."

"Look," Davis said, "Gina said you've been giving her a hard time, so I thought I'd talk to you about it."

Disgusted, Nick said, "Strange, she didn't strike me as the kind of woman who needed someone else to fight her battles."

"She isn't," Davis told him, and his smile was gone. "But she's family now. And I look out for my family."

Nick took the man's measure and slowly nodded. He could understand family loyalty. "I'd do the same."

"Then you'll lighten up on Gina?"

"I'll fire only if fired upon," he said solemnly.

Davis smiled again. "Sounds fair enough to me." He held out his right hand once more, and Nick took it in a firm shake. "Good to meet you, Gunny."

"Same goes, Gunny," Nick said.

But as the other man walked off toward

his own car, Nick's mind was racing. Gina Santini had called in reinforcements. Oh, maybe she hadn't come right out and asked her brother-in-law to talk to him, but she'd probably expected him to. That meant she wasn't retreating, only re-grouping.

She may have won the first battle, but as far as Nick was concerned, the war was still on.

# Three

**F**amily-dinner night at the Santinis' was always interesting. At least one night a week, no matter what else was going on in their lives, the Santinis came together over the dinner table. And for a couple of hours they caught each other up on the news, argued, laughed and ate themselves into a stupor.

Gina glanced around at the faces of her family and smiled to herself. Mama, of course, lonelier since Papa's death two years ago, but still vibrant and deeply involved in whatever her daughters were up to. Then there was Angela, the oldest Santini sister. A widow herself, Angela and her son, Jeremy, had moved back home after her husband's death three years ago. Jeremy was a great kid, Gina thought as her glance slid in his direction. And it was doing him a world of good to have Davis, Marie's new husband, in the family. Jeremy's father hadn't been much good at the "family" thing. He'd made all of their lives miserable, and if anyone here was willing to admit it out loud, they'd have to say that Angela was actually happier as a widow than she had ever been when she was married.

But naturally *no one* would ever admit it.

Then there was Marie. Gina smiled to herself as she looked at the middle Santini sister. Since meeting and falling in love with Davis, Marie had really come into her own. Oh, she was still a great mechanic, and spent most of her time happily involved in some greasy job or other. But there was a sparkle in her eyes and a glow about her that hadn't been there before Davis.

So basically, she told herself with an inward frown, every Santini at the table looked happy as a clam. Except of course, for her.

"I saw your Gunnery Sergeant Paretti today," Davis said, and reached for the bowl of pasta.

Well, *that* came out of nowhere.

Gina looked at him. "He's not *my* anything," she said, and forked up a bite of salad.

"Yeah, well, I had a little talk with him, anyway," her brother-in-law told her. He looked pretty pleased with himself about it, too.

Eyes wide, she hurriedly chewed, swallowed and said, "You *talked* to him? When? Where? What do you mean? What did you say?"

Davis shrugged, smiled at his wife, then looked back at Gina. "To answer your questions in order…after work, at the Staff NCO club, and I just told him you were my sister-in-law and I'd appreciate it if he'd back off."

"Oh, great." She dropped her fork with a clatter and sat back in her chair.

"Wasn't that nice?" Mama asked no one in particular and reached out to pat Davis's hand fondly.

"Nice?" Gina said, staring at her mother. "You think it's nice?"

"What's wrong with you?" Marie demanded. "Davis was just trying to help you out."

"If he wanted to help," Gina said,

glaring at her sister, "then he should have simply run the man down in the street."

"Oh," Angela piped up, "*there's* a plan."

"Run who down?" Eight-year-old Jeremy asked.

"A nice Marine like Davis, dear," Mama told him, and handed him more garlic bread. Unflappable, Mama let *nothing* interfere with dinner.

"No he's not," Gina said quickly.

"Nice?" Mama asked.

"Like Davis," Gina clarified.

"What's the big deal?" Angela asked as she poured her son more milk. "So Davis talked to him. You're overreacting, Gina."

"Big surprise," Marie muttered.

"I am not overreacting," Gina snapped. "How does this look? Now he thinks I went crying to my big brother-in-law wailing for help."

"You did," Marie reminded her, rising to her husband's defense like a lioness defending its den.

"I did not," she argued hotly, and shifted her gaze from Marie to Davis. "Did I ever ask you to talk to the man? Did I plead for your help?"

"No, but..." Davis squirmed in his chair.

Ordinarily Gina might have felt sorry for him, surrounded by women, the only other jolt of testosterone in the room coming from a boy too small to be on his side. But not tonight.

"Cut it out, Gina," Marie said sharply. "Davis was trying to help you, for crying out loud. It's your own fault. All you've done since starting those classes is complain about the man."

Okay, so she'd complained a little. Wasn't that one of the perks of having a family? They were supposed to let you rant and rave. She hadn't noticed them rushing out to buy her new clothes when she complained about her wardrobe.

"Papa would have been pleased with what Davis did for you," Mama said. "Family takes care of family."

Oh, for pity's sake, she made it sound like they were in the Mafia. What's next? We send Nick a dead fish wrapped in newspaper?

"But..." Gina began.

"Davis went out of his way to find this guy, you know. He did you a favor. The least you could do is thank him." Marie stared at her, silently waiting for Gina to do just that.

Five pairs of eyes watched her. She could hear the ticking of the mantel clock in the living room. No one moved. Damn it. Didn't they understand that even though he'd meant well, Davis had just made a complicated situation even more difficult?

In an instant she recalled everything Nick had said to her after their last class. *Spoiled. Pampered. Princess.* Well, now, thanks to Davis's well intentioned meddling, Nick would think himself proved right.

Why was her life suddenly so complicated?

Men, that's why.

First, there had been Richard. A lawyer she'd dated long enough to convince her to take ballroom dancing lessons in order to fit into his social sphere. Unfortunately she'd stopped dating him before her second class. Though a perfectly nice man, they hadn't shared enough chemistry to set off a sparkler.

Sparklers. Fireworks. Skyrockets.

The thought of which brought to mind the new male in her life. Nick Paretti. Her blood hummed in her veins. Her stomach pitched and rolled.

Oh, for Pete's sake.

"Gina!"

Marie's voice dragged her back to the moment at hand.

"You could at least pay attention when we're arguing," her sister said.

"Oh, I'm paying attention," she muttered, then continued, "all I said was that Nick Paretti is a pain in the—"

"Gina." Mama's voice broke in, firmly.

She closed her mouth, sighed then said, "He's a pain in the drain, that's all."

Mama nodded, satisfied.

Jeremy snickered until his mother shushed him. Apparently, he hadn't been fooled by his aunt's quick save.

"I only meant to help," Davis said, looking directly into Gina's eyes.

Instantly she regretted shouting at him.

He *had* meant well. And if you stopped to think about it, it was really very sweet, him rushing in to play big brother. Boy, would she have loved having him around when she was a kid.

"I know," she said, giving him a smile and letting him know he was forgiven. It wasn't his fault she had such conflicting feelings for Nick. Then she forced herself to add, "Thanks, Davis. You're a good brother."

He grinned at her. "Yeah, I think I'm getting the hang of it."

Conversation flowed again, swirling around and past Gina. No one seemed to notice that she wasn't taking part.

"Okay, let's have it," Gina said as they left the dance studio.

"Have what?" Nick glanced up at the starry sky and shrugged deeper into the windbreaker jacket he wore.

"I've been waiting all night," she said, and grabbed his arm to bring him to a stop.

Scowling, he turned his gaze down at her. He should have known they wouldn't be able to go an entire night without an argument. Although, up until now the evening had gone fine. They'd hardly spoken and they'd danced better than ever. Maybe that was the secret to getting along with Gina Santini. No talking.

"Waiting for what?" he asked.

"For you to make some smart remark about my brother-in-law hunting you down on base."

"Oh..." Nick nodded and immediately understood. She was wondering why he hadn't said anything. But the truth was, he'd been doing a lot of thinking since Davis Garvey had spoken to him a few days ago. In fact, he'd been trying to figure out exactly why Gina Santini rubbed him the wrong way more often than not. He'd lost his temper more times since he'd met her than he had in the past five years. And that wasn't like Nick at all.

Then last night the truth had finally dawned on him. Gina reminded him—too much—of his ex-wife. Oh, she didn't look anything like her, and if truth be known, Gina was a helluva lot nicer than Kim had ever been. But there were too many similarities to ignore, too.

Both of them spoiled, used to getting their own ways and not above using their looks to do it. Every time Gina tried to flirt her way out of an argument, Nick's defenses went on full alert. He'd fallen once for a woman with more looks than heart. He wouldn't let it happen again.

As for her brother-in-law's visit, there was no need to say anything about that. If Nick had been in the same position, he would have done the very thing Davis had. In the Paretti household they'd learned one lesson very early in life. Family comes first.

"Forget it," he said finally, and saw wary relief wash over her features.

Obviously, she wanted to believe him, but didn't.

"Why are you being so nice?"

"I can't be nice without an ulterior motive?"

"I don't know."

Well, hell. Good to know she thought he was a complete jerk. "Look, why don't we call a truce for the duration of the lessons?"

"A truce?"

"Yeah. You know, a cease-fire."

"I know what it is, I'm just not sure why you're offering one."

He inhaled sharply and let the cold ocean breeze reach down inside him and quench his budding temper. Even when he was trying to be agreeable, she fought him. "We both want to learn these damned dances, right?"

"Right."

"We don't have to like each other. All we have to do is dance together." There. He couldn't make it plainer than that. "Deal?" He held out his right hand.

She stared at it for a long moment as if it were a snake in striking distance. Then she slipped her hand into his and said, "Deal."

Warmth skittered up from their clasped hands, and Nick released her quickly. Then she flashed him a million-watt smile, and he had to firmly remind himself that it would be easy to resist her charms.

"As long as we're being so friendly," Gina said as they started again for their cars, "maybe you'd like to reconsider entering that competition."

He snorted a laugh. A private truce was one thing. Announcing publicly that he was taking dancing lessons was quite another. "Not a chance, princess."

"So much for a truce," she muttered.

"I'm not entering that contest."

"But we're really getting good," she argued.

"No way," Nick said and shook his head for emphasis.

She took his arm and stepped in close. "You could at least think about it."

Her perfume drifted to him, and he inhaled it deeply. Light, flowery, it seemed to fill his head with images of summer nights. Her hand on his arm felt warm and entirely too good. He didn't dare risk a look at her. No doubt she was wearing her patented, "pouting for prizes" expression. And as much as he'd like to pretend he could easily resist it, he knew darned well it would be tough.

"Gunnery Sergeant Paretti?" A woman called out to him from off to their left.

Nick glanced her way and simply stared at the woman. Good Lord. The new Colonel's wife. A thousand thoughts ran through his head in an instant. Would she know that he and Gina had come from the dance studio? No, he told himself. Close by, there was a theater, the Bayside Seafood Restaurant, an art gallery and a drugstore. They might have been in any of them. Nope. He was in the clear. Relaxing just a bit, he smiled and said, "Mrs. Thornton, ma'am. Good evening."

"Hello," she said and walked closer, smiling warmly at both Gina and him.

Gina.

Oh, man. How could he silently tell his dance partner to keep quiet about what they'd been up to?

"Mrs. Thornton, Gina Santini," he said, unable to avoid introducing the two women.

"Nice to meet you," Gina said.

"Thank you." The Colonel's wife smiled at the two of them again before saying, "My, what a lovely couple you make."

Nick almost choked.

Gina actually chuckled.

"Taking in a movie?" The other woman asked.

Gina opened her mouth, but before she could speak, Nick said, "That's right."

Gina frowned up at him, but he ignored her and slipped his arm around her shoulder. If the Colonel's wife believed he and Gina were a happy couple, then he'd just play along. It was certainly a better option than letting her know the truth.

"Well, I'm so glad I ran into the two of you," Cecelia Thornton said.

"Ma'am?" Hurriedly, Nick tried to think of a way to get Gina and him out of there. But there was no polite way to leave the Colonel's wife standing alone in a parking lot, so he could only hope to escape this meeting unscathed.

"As you know, we're new on base..."

"Yes, ma'am." He shot a glance at Gina. What was she thinking?

"The Colonel and I will be hosting a small get-together at our house in a couple of weeks for the staff NCOs and their wives. A barbecue, if the weather looks fine enough."

Nick nodded. It was customary for a new officer to get to know the noncoms in his command.

"I look forward to it, ma'am." He'd already heard about the coming party and had been planning on making an appearance and then leaving as soon as politely possible. Just like every other single Marine he knew. The married guys always stayed longer at these things, mainly because their wives were enjoying themselves too much to leave.

"I hope you'll attend as Gunnery Sergeant Pa-retti's guest, Gina," the Colonel's wife was saying, and Nick's breath knotted in his chest. Okay, he hadn't expected that. Maybe trying to look like a couple hadn't been such a good idea after all.

"Well..." Gina stalled as she looked up at Nick.

Silently he attempted to tell her to say "thanks, but no thanks." Giving her shoulder a hard squeeze, he tried to give the appearance of a solicitous boyfriend all the while, wiggling his eyebrows and scowling slightly in warning.

She knew what he wanted her to say. He could see it in her eyes. Naturally, though, she didn't say it. Instead, she leaned into him, laid one hand on his chest and smiled at the Colonel's wife. "Thanks so much for inviting me," she said. "Nicky and I are looking forward to it."

Nicky?

His mind blanked out briefly while he enjoyed the play of Gina's fingers against his chest. Oh, she was really burying herself in the part, he thought as she cozied into him. And damn if it didn't feel good, too.

A few more minutes passed while Gina and the Colonel's wife chatted aimlessly. He didn't even hear what was said. Nick's mind whirled with thoughts of murder while he continued to play the good boyfriend.

When the other woman finally strolled off toward the drugstore, Nick grabbed Gina's arm and turned her around to face him. "What was that all about? Didn't you get that I was trying to tell you to say no to the invitation?''

''Of course I got it,'' Gina said, and pulled away from him with a smile. ''You're not that hard to read.''

''Then why?''

''Because, *Nicky,*'' she said, ''something suddenly occurred to me.''

''Yeah…?'' Oh, this didn't bode well for him at all. She looked entirely too sure of herself.

She grinned up at him and pushed her dark-brown curls out of her eyes. Devilment shone in their choc-olaty depths, and he knew he was in for it.

''You didn't want her to know you were taking dance lessons, did you?''

Shoving his hands into his back pockets, he said shortly, ''No, I didn't.''

''That's what I thought,'' she said, nodding slowly.

"Now, why'd you agree to go the party?"

"So that I would have a good position to bargain from."

Here it comes, he thought, and tried to brace for whatever was coming. Hell, he'd been in combat. Surely he could take whatever Gina Santini could dish out. "Bargain for what?"

"I'll go to that party with you—" she paused and smiled "—and you'll enter the dance contest with me."

So much for bracing himself. "Whoa," he said, and held up one hand. "Back up and regroup."

She shook her head. "Excuse me? I don't speak Marine."

Over the roaring in his ears, he said, "Trot that past me again, slower this time."

Now she grinned. "No problem. I

don't blow your cover with the Colonel's wife, and you enter the contest with me.''

''That's blackmail,'' he said, and silently congratulated himself on the even tone of his voice.

''I prefer the word *extortion,*'' she responded, still smiling. ''It sounds so much...friendlier.''

He drew his head back and stared down at the woman who'd trapped him so neatly. Oh, he hadn't given her nearly enough credit.

''Of course,'' Gina said, and her smile broadened, ''you could tell Mrs. Thornton that we've broken up. But then I could attend the Colonel's party on my own, since I've been invited, and tell every Marine there about how we met while you were taking Fred Astaire lessons.''

''Lady,'' he said tightly, ''why are you trying to ruin my life?''

"Don't take it so hard, General," she said, patting his arm. "Who knows? We might even win."

Damn it. He was caught and he knew it. She had him over the proverbial barrel. He had to choose between being humiliated in front of strangers—or his friends. Victory was plainly written in her expression, but before he conceded defeat, he had to know something.

"Why are you so interested in that competition, anyway?" he demanded.

Gina gave him a smile that sent shock waves rippling through his body. "It's a *contest,*" she said, as if that was explanation enough. Then she added with a shrug, "I like winning."

"Okay, that works for me. I like winning, too," he said tightly. "And, princess, I don't often lose."

# Four

"**W**hat's that supposed to mean?" Gina asked as she took a step back, still keeping her gaze on him.

"It means, blackmailing a Marine isn't always the wisest course of action."

His blue eyes narrowed into dangerous slits, and his jaw was clenched so tightly the muscle there ticked with the regularity of a heartbeat. He was trying to look intimidating. And doing a pretty darn good job of it, too. Unfortunately for him, she'd already spent three weeks in his company and she knew for a fact that no matter how angry he became, Nick Paretti remained a gentleman.

"You know what?" she asked with a shake of her head. "That terrify-the-troops expression you're wearing doesn't scare me."

He groaned, shoved one hand along the side of his head and muttered something she didn't quite catch. Probably for the best, she thought. Heaven knew they'd be arguing again soon enough.

"What will scare you off?" he asked tightly.

She *should* be scared off by the way he made her feel. Unfortunately, what she felt only made her want to feel more. "You're making too big a deal out of this," she told him and reached out to lay one hand on his forearm.

"Pardon me," he said, and rubbed the

back of his neck. "I've never been blackmailed before."

"It won't be that bad," Gina said, and let her hand drop from the tense muscles of his forearm.

"Maybe not for you."

For goodness' sake. This wasn't the end of the world. It was a dance contest. "Honestly, Nick. You'd think I'd asked you to go up against terrorists with a water pistol."

For a minute he looked hopeful. "That I could do."

Gina laughed, and he gave her a reluctant smile as he shook his head.

"Fine," he said. "We compete."

"Excellent." Still smiling, she dipped one hand into her purse, searching for her car keys.

"But," he said, "if we're going to enter this stupid contest, then we're damn sure gonna win it."

"My plan exactly," she told him, frowning as her fingers burrowed futilely through the accumulated junk in her bag.

"And that means extra practicing."

"Huh?" She shot him a look.

"Three times a week isn't going to cut it, Gina. The way I see it, we'll have to practice practically every night we don't have class."

"That much?"

"Any Marine can tell you, you have to drill and drill to get it right."

"So this is now a military maneuver?" she asked.

"Whatever works."

"I really hadn't thought about extra practicing," she admitted, and pulled a fistful of flotsam from her purse. "Here," she said, handing it to him. "Hold this."

He cupped his hands, and she started piling things in his palms. "What in the...?"

"I guess it'll be all right, but I have school on Friday nights."

Staring down at the growing pile in his hands, Nick said, "Hey, if you don't have the time..."

"I'll find the time," she assured him as she dropped a few more items into his cupped hands. "I guess we could practice at my apartment..."

"Is there enough room?"

"Well, it's not the Harbor View Ballroom," she admitted, "but it'll do."

Although, she thought suddenly, the small garage apartment she'd inherited when Marie married Davis and moved to a bigger place would seem even smaller with this mountain of a man in it. Maybe this wasn't such a brilliant idea. Maybe she was only setting herself up for some real trouble here. After all, with the way her body reacted to his when they were close, too much privacy could be a dangerous thing.

But before she could explore that thought any further, Nick said, "Ya know, this is amazing."

"Huh? What?" She dropped her cell phone, a candy bar and a pocket screwdriver onto the top of the pile he was holding.

"This," he said, hefting the collection in his hands a bit higher. "I've never known a woman who carried around half a submarine sandwich, a full-size flashlight and a travel Battleship game in her purse."

Defensive, she said, "I didn't get to finish my lunch today, parking lots are dark and my nephew *likes* playing Battleship." At last! She hooked her finger through the ring of keys that had been hiding in a wad of tissues and held them aloft like she would a gold medal at the Olympics.

"That purse must weigh in as much as a Marine's full pack."

"What?" Tucking her keys into the pocket of her pale blue sweater, she scooped her belongings out of his hands and back into her purse. Small skitters of heat swept up along her arm and dazzled her heart as her fingertips brushed across his palm.

He stared at her. "As little as you are, I'm surprised the weight of that purse doesn't just topple you over."

She hiked the straps higher on her shoulder and settled the familiar weight against her hip. "I'm small, but I'm tough."

Nick gave her a long, slow look that seemed to sizzle through her blood like a line of flames. "I noticed."

Oh, yeah. She might be in some serious

trouble here. But it was too late to back out now. This whole thing was her idea. If she called off entering the contest, he'd want to know why, and she couldn't very well tell him that she didn't trust herself around him.

Besides, she admitted silently, she didn't want to call it off.

"Look," she said abruptly, suddenly needing a little space, "come by my house tomorrow about seven, and we can talk about practice times, okay?"

"All right," he agreed, and opened the car door for her after she'd unlocked it. As she slid in, he asked, "You going to tell me where you live?"

"Oh!" Automatically she reached for her bag again. "I'll write it down for you."

He leaned one arm on the roof of the car and bent down. "Forget it," he said. "Just tell me. I'm not strong enough to watch you go through all that junk again just yet.''

Frowning, she stared up at him. ''Are you this pleasant with *all* women? Or is it just me?''

He thought about it for a moment or two, then nodded. ''Actually, it's just you.''

''Wonderful.''

''Hey,'' he told her, with what might have been a glimmer of a smile, ''blackmailers shouldn't expect to be *liked.*''

A quick stab of guilt poked at Gina's insides, but she fought it down. Okay, so she probably shouldn't have blackmailed him. But he'd started it by lying to his Colonel's wife. All he'd had to do to end this whole thing was tell the truth.

There. She felt better already.

''All right,'' she said, ''we'll play it your way.''

''If we were playing it my way, princess,'' he said softly, ''we wouldn't be doing this competition thing at all.''

She took a deep breath and blew it out slowly. ''Look, I don't know about you, but I can't stay here and argue all night. I have an early class tomorrow.''

''And I have to work, so give me your address and we'll call it a night.''

She did. Then slammed the car door, making him jump back out of range, turned the key in the ignition and put the gearshift in drive. Only then did she notice he was still standing there, watching her.

Rolling down the window, she looked up at him with exasperation and asked, ''What?''

''Nothing.'' He shoved his hands into his pockets and shrugged. ''Just waiting to make sure you get on your way safely.''

A small spurt of warmth shot through

her. Even though he argued with her over anything and everything, he watched out for her in a dark parking lot. An argumentative Nick she could handle. If he started being nice… "Are you this considerate of all blackmailers?" she asked.

"Nope," he said, looking directly into her eyes. "Just you."

Oh, boy.

"Well," she said, letting her gaze slide away from his, "thanks. See you tomorrow."

"Seven it is."

Leaving it at that, Gina stepped on the gas pedal and left Nick Paretti standing alone in the parking lot.

"So," First Sergeant Dan Mahoney asked, "you up for some pool tonight?"

Nick looked up from the pile of papers he was going through only long enough to glance at his friend. Dan was practically rubbing his palms together in anticipation. And no wonder. Last week he'd won twenty bucks from Nick at pool. "No, thanks, I'm busy."

"With what?" Dan eased down into the chair opposite Nick's desk and propped his feet up onto the corner. "Or should I ask, with *who?*"

Grumbling under his breath, Nick looked at the other man. "What makes you think it's a *who?* I'm behind on these inventory sheets, I've got a world of paperwork stacking up behind them, plus I've got to take the platoon on a twenty-mile run day after tomorrow. Does that sound like I have time to play pool?"

"Sounds like you *need* to play pool," Dan said, smiling.

What he needed was to be able to get Gina Santini out of his mind. But it didn't look like that would be happening anytime soon.

Nick sighed and leaned back in his chair. Tossing his pencil onto the desktop, he lifted his arms over his head and stretched, easing kinks out of muscles that would never get used to sitting behind a desk. He hadn't joined the Corps to be a desk jockey. Give him men to train, battles to fight or miles to run and he was a happy man. Sit him down with a pencil and a stack of mindless paperwork and you had a man on the edge.

Which was exactly why he'd never give in to his father's request to leave the Corps and join the family business. Nick Paretti was no businessman. He was a Marine and would stay a Marine until they pried him out of the Corps with a crowbar.

But at least while he was concentrating on the weaponry inventory lists, he had less time to think about Gina Santini and what he'd gotten himself into. It was hard enough to ignore the flash of heat between them when they were in a dance class surrounded by people. What would it be like when it was just the two of them? Alone in her apartment...?

He never should have agreed, he thought. He should have called her bluff. She probably wouldn't have gone to the Colonel's wife. But then again, she might have...

"Nick!"

"What?" He blinked and stared at his friend.

"Hey," Dan said on a laugh, "if I want to be ignored, I'll get married."

"Very funny," Nick told him and sat up, reaching for his pencil again. Dan Mahoney, king of the one-night stands, married? That'd be the day.

"You know what you need, Gunny?" Dan said as he pushed himself up from the chair.

"I have a feeling you're about to tell me."

"Damn straight." Dan planted his palms on the desktop and leaned in. "You need to get off base occasionally and find a woman."

Right. Just what he needed. He already had one woman too many in his life. Nick snorted and shook his head. "Contrary to what you might think, a woman is not the answer to every problem."

"Maybe not," Dan said as he started for the door, "but they're sure as hell good company while you're looking for the answer."

"Yeah," Nick muttered when he was alone again, "but what if the woman *is* the problem?"

Gina had daydreamed through her statistics class, doodled through accounting and yawned through computer science.

All in all, a stellar performance by the world's most reluctant and probably oldest, college sophomore.

Sighing, she dropped her books and her purse onto the coffee table, kicked off her shoes and walked barefoot into her tiny kitchen. Every muscle in her body was tired. She'd worked a five-hour shift for the catering company and then reported for an afternoon of classes and now she was pooped. Opening up the fridge, she grabbed a jar of iced tea, unscrewed the cap and took a long swallow before closing the refrigerator and leaning back against the counter.

She just wasn't cut out for college, she thought, disgusted. She wanted to be working. And not for Sally Simon's Catering Club. She wanted to build her own business. She wanted to plan splashy, fun events. Hire caterers with more imagination than experience. Build both a business and a name for herself. But she'd promised her father that she'd get the darned degree, and that's just what she would do. And when that task was finished, she could get busy on the other promise she'd made him the night he died.

Two-year-old memories crowded into her mind, and Gina swallowed them back with a swig of tea. Tears stung her eyes, and she blinked them away. Papa had been gone two years, and she could still see his face, hear his voice, as clearly as she had on that last night.

Her fingers tightened around the cold bottle of tea as she resolutely dragged her mind from thoughts of the past. She had more pressing things to think about at the moment. Nick would be here any minute. Her stomach flip-flopped. And that quick spark of anticipation she'd just felt would be completely ignored, she warned herself.

"Giiiinnnaaa..." Her mother's voice cut into her thoughts and not for the first time Gina had to marvel at a woman who could be heard through closed doors and windows. Never let it be said that Mama used a telephone when shouting out the kitchen door would work just as well.

Crossing the living room, Gina threw open her front door, stepped out onto the narrow landing and called, "What is it?" before she looked down to see Nick standing shoulder to shoulder with Mama as both of them looked up at her.

Even from a distance she felt as though she was being drawn into the blue depths of his eyes, and something inside her didn't mind the thought of that at all.

"Your young man is here," her mother said, and Gina groaned, relieved that it was dark enough outside to hide the stamp of embarrassment on her face. But Mama wasn't finished. "He didn't know about the garage apartment, so he came here, and I invited him for some coffee and pie. Why don't you come down, Gina?"

Oh for heaven's sake, she thought, and let her gaze slide to Nick's face. He actually looked amused.

"Gina?" Mama shook her head and, in an aside to Nick, said loudly enough for the neighbors to hear, "Sometimes she daydreams and forgets what's going on, but you'll get used to that."

Gina opened her mouth to argue the point, but decided against having a shouting match with her mother. Mama would win hands down, anyway. Hurrying down the stairs, Gina waited until she was at the foot of the porch steps before saying, "I wasn't daydreaming, and he's not my young man, he's my dancing partner."

Well, good. That wiped the amused smile off his face.

"Ah, dancing," Mama said, and half turned to give Nick the once-over again. "Gina's papa, he was a wonderful dancer."

"Was he?" Nick murmured politely.

"And so light on his feet for a big man," Mama was saying. Her eyes went soft and dreamy, and Gina knew her mother was remembering the nights when she and Papa had swayed together in the darkened living room to the rhythm of Frank Sinatra's smooth-as-silk voice pouring from the stereo.

Gina sighed a little, recalling all the times she and her sisters had hidden in the shadowy hallway to watch their parents dance. She'd never said anything about it, but there'd been a magical feel to those moments. Almost as if the world stood still while Mama and Papa moved together in perfect harmony. She could still remember the warm sense of… rightness that had filled her then. Secure in the knowledge of her parents' love for each other and for their daughters, Gina had wanted the same thing for herself.

But she wasn't a child hiding in doorways anymore, and now she knew that responsibilities had to come before dreams of love.

"Thanks for the offer, Mama," she said, bringing Marianne Santini back from the past, "but Nick and I have got some talking to do."

"You can't talk over pie?"

Mama was never one to give up easily. "Maybe later, all right?"

"Fine, fine," her mother said, and waved them off. "But you, what did you say your name was again?"

‘‘Nick Paretti, ma’am,’’ he said, and shook the hand she offered.

‘‘Hmmm.’’ Mama looked at Gina knowingly. ‘‘A nice *Italian* boy. Well, don’t be a stranger.’’

‘‘Oh, for Heaven’s sake.’’ Grabbing Nick’s hand, Gina tugged him toward the apartment stairs. As she hurried him along, she muttered, ‘‘Run for your life, General, before she has time to order wedding invitations and book the church.’’

# Five

Nick followed Gina up the stairs and would have sworn he could feel Mrs. Santini's interested stare boring into his back as he went. He shrugged deeper into his olive-green windbreaker and tried to ignore the sensation of being measured by a maternal eye.

Since his divorce, Nick had purposely avoided any entanglements with the kind of woman who would eventually expect a marriage proposal. And now, because of one little accident with a punch bowl, he'd been thrown into shark-infested waters.

Dance lessons. Why hadn't the damned Major just arranged a nice, quiet firing squad instead? It would have been the kinder thing to do.

At the top of the stairs, Gina paused for less than a heartbeat, then glanced back at him and said, "Come on in." She stepped aside to let him enter, and as soon as he did, his gaze swept across the place. Small, but neat, it looked what some people would call "cozy." There was an overstuffed sofa with a few colorful throw pillows, two chairs and a couple of tables where lamps with pale shades sat glowing in the darkness. On one wall was a small entertainment center, where stacks of books were piled haphazardly beside a small television and a compact stereo.

From where he stood, he could see directly into the galley-size kitchen, and a closed door to the right told him where her bedroom probably was. His gaze lingered on that closed door for a moment or two before he turned his head to look down at her.

"Nice place," he said, tucking his hands into his pockets.

"Thanks," Gina muttered, then closed the front door and moved past him into the room.

She wore tight, faded blue jeans, soft from hundreds of washings and the damn things fit her like a second skin. Her bright-green T-shirt had a V neck that was just low enough to interest a man, and her bare feet made this little meeting seem a bit more…intimate, somehow.

And after that near kiss the other night, he was a man on the edge. A rush of heat surged through him. Mistake, he thought.

Big mistake. They should have met somewhere public. Like maybe the Rose Bowl.

She walked to the sofa and sat down, curling one leg beneath her. Glancing up at him, she waved him to a seat and said, "Look, I'm sorry about Mama—"

"Forget it," Nick interrupted and thought about joining her on the sofa before taking a seat in one of the chairs, deliberately keeping some distance between them. This was the first time they'd been together without the safety net of a few other couples around. Well, except for the parking lot, and that sure as hell didn't count.

Outside, with a cold ocean breeze keeping them both wrapped up in jackets, there wasn't much chance that either of them would let down their guard. Here…a *whole* different story.

"I don't know why she does that,"

Gina said, thankfully disrupting his train of thought.

Good. They could talk about their mothers. A subject guaranteed to keep thoughts of sex at bay.

"I'm Italian, too," Nick reminded her. "Trust me. Your mom and mine would get along great."

Gina shook her head, then pushed her hair back from her face with a swipe of her hand. He didn't want to know why that movement suddenly looked so...sensual.

"Is it an Italian thing?" she asked. "Or a mother thing?"

He shrugged and leaned back in the chair, stretching his legs out in front of him, pretending to be more relaxed than he felt. "Embarrassing your children is a mother thing universally, I think. Italian mothers just do it with a little more gusto."

Gina laughed shortly, and Nick enjoyed the sound of it.

Which should have sent off more warning bells in his brain.

"Mama will never give up, I guess," she said.

"If she's like my mom," he said, "she wants grandchildren."

"She's already got a grandson," Gina complained. "My sister Angela's son, Jeremy. Plus my other sister, Marie, just got married, so she's bound to have one or two kids. Why doesn't she work on them?"

"You're a challenge," Nick said with a commiserating smile. Heck, he knew just what she was putting up with. He heard it often enough himself when he went home on leave.

His mother wouldn't rest easy until he was married again and had two or three kids. Which meant she'd never be resting easy, poor woman.

"That's just it," Gina said. "I'm not a challenge. I've already told Mama that I'm not going to get married."

"Until…" he said, waiting for her to finish what had to be an uncompleted sentence.

She looked at him. "Until never."

No way did he believe that. A woman who looked like Gina was *not* destined to live her life alone. Sooner or later she would snag some guy who'd spend the rest of his life trying to ease away her pouts.

Still, she'd surprised him. And that didn't happen often. He wasn't sure how their meeting about dancing practice had evolved into talking about life and whatnot, but he was too interested now to change direction.

He'd always thought of himself as a

fairly good judge of character. Came from being in the Corps, he guessed. After a few years you got to the point where you could look at a new recruit and know whether he was going to make it or not. As for women…well, he'd learned his lessons the hard way, courtesy of his ex-wife.

Never again would he be fooled by a pretty face and a few sighs in the darkness. He knew now that women wanted one thing from him. Marriage and access to his family's money. Nick Paretti alone wasn't much of a prize. But the Paretti Computer Corporation? Now *there* was a worthy scalp to be taken.

"You don't want to get married? Have kids?" he asked, his disbelief coloring his tone.

"Do you?" she countered.

All right, he'd give a little information to get a little. "Tried it once," he said off-handedly. ‘‘Marriage, that is, not kids.’’

‘‘What happened?’’

What didn’t? Nick shrugged and gave her the short answer. ‘‘Turns out she wasn’t interested in being a Marine wife after all.’’

Gina just looked at him, confusion etched into her features. ‘‘She married a Marine and then complained about it?’’

Actually, Nick thought, she’d married a Marine hoping he’d leave the Corps and go to work with his father. As soon as she’d found out differently, she’d lost interest. Kim hadn’t wanted to live on a Marine’s salary. She’d expected him to draw on the family money, and when he didn’t…

He pushed himself to his feet and wandered across the room to the wide, front window that overlooked the driveway and the street beyond. Nick still remembered the pain of realizing Kim had never really loved him. She'd looked at him and seen a bank balance. Nothing more.

Gina was still watching him; he felt her gaze on him as surely as he would have her touch. He knew she wanted to hear more. Knew curiosity was probably killing her. And for some weird reason he found himself wanting to tell her the rest of it.

Staring through the glass, he focused blindly on the soft glow of streetlamps, the moonlight drifting down from the cloud-scattered sky and the tree limbs dipping and swaying in the wind. "She thought she could change me," he said. "Wanted me to resign from the Marines. Go to work for the family business."

"Family business?" she asked.

"Paretti Computers."

There was a long pause, then Gina said, "You're *that* Paretti?"

"*I'm* not," he said, as he had so many times before. "My father is."

"Wow."

He almost smiled. Typical. The minute someone found out about his family—and to be fair, it wasn't only the women—they treated him differently. Everyone wanted something. Everyone looked at him and saw, not Nick, but opportunity.

Gina wouldn't be any different.

"Stupid woman."

Surprised again, he turned his head and looked at her. "What?"

"Your ex-wife." Gina smiled and shook her head. "Well, come on. Anyone with half an eye can see you're a Marine right down to your bones. The woman had to be an idiot to think you'd leave what you obviously love."

Hmm.

Something stirred inside him, and he wondered if he'd been right in his first assessment of Gina. Maybe she and Kim weren't so alike after all. And then again, maybe Gina just played the game better than Kim had. Say all the right things, keep the man off balance, then, when he's teetering on the edge of sanity, give him that one last push and wham. Caught.

"My father had an auto garage," Gina was saying, and he stopped thinking and started listening.

Her voice went soft, softer than he'd ever heard it before, and the expression on her face told him a lot about how she felt about her father. "Had?" he asked.

Her gaze caught his, and he noted the quick sheen of tears fill her eyes before she blinked them back.

"He died about two years ago."

"I'm sorry," Nick said, and meant it. No matter how crazy his own dad made him, bugging him to leave the Corps, wanting him to settle down and raise a family—Nick couldn't really imagine the world without the old man in it.

She gave him a brief, sad smile. "Thanks. But, anyway, what I was going to say was, when he died, Mama and Angela and I wanted to sell the shop." Gina stood up and walked around from behind the coffee table and crossed the room to the entertainment center. There, she punched the power button on the stereo and began to thumb through a small pile of CDs. "I'm not sure why, now. Yet at the time, it seemed like the right thing to do. But Marie fought us."

"Why?" he asked, and noticed his voice was as soft as hers. As though they were both afraid to break this spell between them. For the first time since he'd known her, they were talking. *Really* talking.

She threw him a quick glance and smiled. "Because she's like you."

Intriguing statement. ‘‘How’s that?’’

Gina shrugged. ‘‘She’s a mechanic, right down to her bones. Tools and cars are to her what the Corps is to you. Papa taught her everything she knows, and that shop was as important to her as it was to him.’’

Strange, that a woman he’d spent the last few weeks arguing with knew him better than the woman who’d professed to love him. He watched her and felt a stirring deep within him. She spoke again, and he tried to focus on what she was saying, not on what she was making him feel.

‘‘We had as much chance of getting Marie out of that shop as your ex-wife had of getting you out of the Marines.’’ She selected a CD, opened the case and loaded up the stereo. ‘‘And about as much right to try.’’

Surprises, he thought. Gina Santini was

just chock-full of surprises. A part of him wanted to believe that she meant everything she was saying. But the more logical part—the part that had been protecting him from more pain ever since Kim left—warned him that she was probably only saying what she thought he wanted to hear.

And damned if he didn't want to hear it.

A slow swell of music drifted up into the room. Horns and piano were joined by Tony Bennett's smooth voice as he sang about black magic and spells and all of the things Nick was beginning to experience firsthand.

Dim lighting, romantic music, just the two of them…a warning signal sprang into life in his brain. Reacting to it, he cleared his throat, tried to shrug off the sudden intimacy between them and said, "Okay, you've heard my story. Now it's your turn. Why are you so uninterested in marriage? Don't tell me you, too, have an ex littering the past."

"No," she said, and walked toward him, her steps unconsciously moving to the sensual rhythm of the music filling the air. His body tightened, and his mouth went dry. Damn, if they could bottle Gina Santini's explosive appeal, they'd have a far-more-powerful weapon than a plain, old A-bomb.

"No ex's," she said and shook her hair back from her face.

"Then why?" It wasn't easy concentrating on the conversation at hand when all he wanted to do was grab her and kiss her senseless, but he gave it his all.

Gina looked up into his eyes as she came closer. "I thought about it," she admitted. In fact, she'd thought of little else for a long time. She wasn't so different from her sisters. She'd dreamed of finding one man to love for a lifetime. Of having lots of kids and a dog and, heck, maybe even the prerequisite station wagon. She'd wanted the whole cliché.

But things were different now. Now she had to think about someone other than herself.

"And?" he prompted.

"I don't want to depend on someone else," she said simply. "I want to take care of myself and—" She broke off and finished lamely, "I just think it's better this way, that's all."

He shook his head. "You'll change your mind."

"Really," she said. "And you won't?"

"Nope."

"And what makes you think I will?"

His gaze swept her up and down, and every inch of her skin tingled as if he was sliding his fingertips along her flesh.

When he finally looked directly into her eyes, he said, "No offense, Gina, you just don't seem like the go-it-alone type to me."

"Why's that?" she asked, drawing her head back and staring at him.

"Hell, look at you," he said.

"What?" She glanced down at herself, then looked back at him.

"Every move you make is designed to drive a man nuts," he said.

She frowned at him. "What are you talking about?"

He shoved one hand across the top of his head and gave her a half smile that lit up his eyes and did strange and wonderful things to her insides. "Hell, princess, just watching you walk across a room is enough to do most men in."

Something inside her trembled slightly.

"Flirting is second nature to you," he added.

Okay, she knew that. But flirting with a man and marrying him were two different things.

He shook his head slowly. "There is no way you're going to convince me you want to lead a celibate life."

Celibate? Gina laughed, then laughed harder at the expression on his face. He looked, she thought, what her mother would call "flabbergasted." Honest to Pete. Because she had no plans to get married, that meant she'd have to sign up for the vestal virgin program?

"What's so funny?"

"You," she said, finally catching her breath again. Planting both hands on her hips, she continued, "I didn't say I was going to join a convent. I said I didn't want to get married." Still chuckling, she added, "Geez, what century do you live in?"

He gave her a twisted, uncomfortable

smile. "Fine. You'll have a string of lovers, then. Oh, very safe way to live."

The bubbles of laughter in her chest flattened out abruptly. So, Gina thought, she was either a nun, a wife, or a tramp. A flash of heat rose up within her and she gave in to it. Insulted, she said, "Nobody said anything about a 'string' of lovers, either."

"Well what exactly do you mean?" His voice was tight with barely restrained anger.

What the heck did *he* have to be mad about?

"Why does it matter to you?" she asked hotly.

"It doesn't," he snapped, and moved in closer.

"Good," she told him, and took a step toward him, too. "Because it doesn't have anything to do with you."

"I know that," Nick grumbled. "It's none of my business what you do."

"Darn right," she snapped, tilting her head back to look up into blue eyes that glittered and shone in the lamplight. Every nerve in her body felt alive and tingling. "I can live my life any way I want to."

"Go ahead."

"I will."

He grabbed her shoulders, his fingers branding her flesh right through the fabric of her T-shirt. He pulled her closely to him, and her breasts flattened against his chest. Bending his head down to hers, he nearly growled, "There's nothing between us."

"Absolutely nothing," she agreed, licking suddenly dry lips. The air in the room felt thinner; she struggled to draw breath.

He held her tighter to him, and a hard,

throbbing ache settled low in her body, turning her knees to water and her mind to mush. How had this happened so quickly? she wondered. Then again, maybe it wasn't quick.

She knew darned well they'd been building toward this moment since the first night they'd met. The moment she'd first stepped into his arms, there'd been electricity between them. Like the sense of anticipation that hovers in the air just before a thunderstorm and lightning hits the earth. It was there. The heat, the magic. All of it waiting for the right time to explode.

All of the arguments. All of the tension that had simmered between them the past several weeks. It was all foreplay. She'd known it the other night when he'd almost kissed her. When she'd wanted him to kiss her.

"This is stupid," he muttered, moving

his gaze across her face like a dying man searching for a glimpse of Heaven.

"More than stupid," she whispered, reaching up to touch his face, smoothing her fingertips along his jawline. "Ridiculous."

"And dangerous," he added as he moved his hands to her back, letting his right hand slide down her spine to the curve of her behind. "Don't forget *dangerous.*"

She gasped, closed her eyes and said, "Can't forget the danger." She silently congratulated herself on getting her voice to work, despite the huge knot in her throat. Breathe, Gina, she told herself. Don't forget to breathe.

"If we do this, we'll regret it," he told her, locking his gaze with hers.

"Undoubtedly," Gina said tightly, and knew that if they didn't, she would regret that even more.

"'But if we don't, it'll kill me,'' Nick admitted.

"Me, too,'' she said breathlessly. Opening her eyes again to look up at him, she felt herself being drawn into the blue depths of his eyes and knew she wanted nothing more at the moment than to let go and simply feel everything that was exploding inside her.

But she knew, too, the decision would be hers. From the tension in his body and the hard set of his jaw, Gina realized that he was letting her make the call. If she turned him away, he'd let it go, and this magic would end here. Now. She'd never know what it was to unleash the lightning. And she'd spend the rest of her life wondering what might have been.

The thought of that dragged a groan from her throat, and his arms tightened around her. Her decision had been made during their first dance. She knew that now. That's why she'd fought so hard against him. Complained so much about him. He'd touched her more than any other man she'd ever known. Made her feel, even when she didn't want to. Made her want him when she knew it would be safer not to.

"Gina?" he asked, and his voice was hoarse with need and the tight restraint he was keeping on the desire obviously pulsing through him.

Reaching up, she laced her fingers behind his head and pulled him down to her. When his mouth was just a breath away from hers, she whispered, "No regrets, General. No matter what?"

"No matter what," he agreed, and his breath brushed across her face.

"Then kiss me, Nick, before I go crazy."

He nodded, muttered, "Ooh-rah!" then claimed her lips in a kiss that flashed through both of them with the white-hot brilliance of summer lightning.

# Six

Nick held her even tighter and knew it still wasn't enough. He needed to feel all of her pressed to him. He needed to know what her skin felt like beneath his palms. He needed to bury himself deep inside her and feel her body cradling his.

Since the moment he'd first laid eyes on her, he'd wanted Gina Santini. A hard thing for a man who'd sworn off women to admit, but she got to him. Got to him on so many different levels he wasn't even sure of all of them himself.

But just looking into her wide, brown eyes was enough to stoke the fires that were always smoldering inside him, and for right now, that was all he needed to know. His mouth moved on hers again, his tongue tracing the line of her lips until he'd teased her into opening for him. And then he slipped into her warmth, his tongue sweeping across the inside of her mouth, tasting her, swallowing her sighs, taking her breath as his own.

She groaned softly, and as their tongues met Nick tightened his grip around her middle, crushing her to him. Her arms came around his neck, her fingers pressing into his shoulders, his back. He felt the imprint of each of her fingers even through the damned windbreaker he'd never taken off.

Tearing his mouth from hers, he held her as he dipped his head to lay down a pathway of kisses along her throat and lower, onto the curve of her collarbone and the vee of flesh that had tantalized him from the minute he'd arrived tonight.

"Oh, Nick," she whispered, and let her head fall back as she swayed in his arms.

"More," he muttered thickly, moving one hand up and around, to cup and fondle one of her breasts. She arched into him, gasping his name, and he looked into her face, reveling in the flush of color sweeping her cheeks and the glazed shine in her eyes.

His fingers slid beneath the edge of her collar and dipped low, pulling at the stretchy fabric until he had access to the small, perfect breast hidden from him by a pale-lavender lace bra. Nick smiled to himself as his thumb and forefinger tweaked her hardened nipple through the fragile barrier separating him from her flesh. Her nipple peaked at his attentions, and Gina groaned again, deeper this time as she tightened her grip on his shoulders.

"I want to see you," he whispered. "I want to taste you. All of you."

"Oh, my," she said on a throaty breath, then added, "I want...I want..."

He knew what she wanted. The same thing he did.

Nick bent his head and kissed the top of her breast and felt the shiver that wracked her body. He smiled against her skin and tugged back the edge of her bra just far enough to allow him to draw his tongue across her breast and close—so close—to her nipple that she shuddered violently and clutched at his shoulders in anticipation.

"Nick," she whispered, and paused only long enough to lick her lips. "Nick, kiss me. Kiss me there."

He grinned and admitted, "I'm tryin', honey, but all this material's in the way."

Nodding, she straightened up and took a shaky step backward. Then she yanked at the hem of her shirt and tugged it up and over her head. In the next instant Nick shrugged out of his windbreaker, then tore off his T-shirt and tossed it to the floor.

Their gazes locked, Gina reached for the front clasp of her bra. Nick stopped her by covering her hands with his own.

"Let me," he said softly.

A moment passed, then she swallowed hard and gave him a jerky nod.

He moved in close again, sliding his fingers up and under the clasp. Gina swayed a little, and when he unsnapped her bra, she grabbed at him, her fingers digging into his upper arms.

Smiling, Nick slowly skimmed his palms up, along her rib cage and under the wispy lace that lay open to his touch. He sighed in satisfaction as he cupped her breasts in his palms, his thumbs caressing the hardened tips of her nipples. Gina moaned and closed her eyes, but kept her iron-like grip on his arms.

Again and again, his fingers toyed with her sensitive skin. She twisted in his grasp, her hips arching toward him as she instinctively gave herself over to the building need.

Perfect, he thought, admiring her small, full breasts even as he slowly bent down to take first one nipple and then the other into his mouth. He tasted her, running the tip of his tongue across the pebbly surface. He teased her, never letting the sensations end, keeping his fingers busy on one breast while his mouth devoured the other. He suckled her, pulling at her flesh with lips and the edges of his teeth until both he and Gina trembled from the pounding need thrumming inside.

And still it wasn't enough. He wanted

it all. He wanted to know all of her. Intimately. He wanted to touch and explore every inch of her body, and even that wouldn't be enough.

Slowly he sank to his knees in front of her, and Gina's hands slid from his upper arms to his shoulders, her grasp still strong. Her fingers digging into his flesh.

"What are you—"

"Shhh," he whispered, and let his hands drop to the button of her jeans. When it was undone, he pulled down the zipper.

"Nick…"

He didn't talk. Couldn't have, even if he'd tried. His throat tight, his mouth dry, he knew only need and the driving force to meet it.

Sliding his hands beneath the waistband of her jeans, he pushed them down, over her hips, along her thighs until they were puddled at her feet. Then he reached back up to her panties, the tiny swatch of lavender lace fabric that was all that lay between him and what he craved so desperately.

"Nick," Gina said, her voice hardly more than a whispered gasp. "I need you to—"

"I know, baby," he assured her and heard the tight gravelly sound of his own voice. "I know just what you need."

His fingers slid beneath the tiny strip of elastic on her panties, and in an instant they, too, were lying at her feet. She stepped out of her clothes and sighed as Nick ran his palms up the length of her legs, skimming across her skin with a heated, gentle touch that torched the flames burning within them both.

He leaned forward then and kissed her flat abdomen, letting his tongue slide across her flesh until her hips moved in his grasp and he felt her short fingernails digging into his shoulders. Dipping his head, he went lower, skimming his mouth along her body, trailing warm, damp kisses across the tops of her thighs, then stopping just at the edge of the triangle of dark-brown curls guarding her center.

Her knees buckled, and Nick instantly cupped her bottom in his palms, steadying her even as his fingers kneaded her tender flesh. "I've got you, princess."

"Nick," she said softly, "the bedroom, let's go into the bedroom."

"Not yet," he said, and brushed another kiss against her abdomen.

She shivered. "If I don't lie down, I'm gonna fall down," she told him on a choked-off laugh.

"Not yet you're not," he assured her, "but soon."

Then he dipped his head and claimed a different kiss.

Gina cried out his name and clutched at him frantically.

Holding her tightly, he opened his mouth and took her, his tongue exploring the intimate details of her body while she shuddered in his grasp.

Gina's world rocked around her. Sensation after sensation rippled up and through her body, and her mind rushed to try to keep up. But it was too much. Too much of everything. Brain reeling, body burning, she simply held on to him as if he were the only stable point in a suddenly shaky universe.

He swiped his tongue across her flesh, and Gina instinctively opened her legs wider for him. Again and again, he tasted her, his tongue doing things to her body she never would have dreamed possible. Gently but determinedly he pushed her along the edge of madness. Driving her up and up and up until she felt as though without his hold on her she might float straight through the roof and into the night sky.

It felt so good, so…unbelievable, she never wanted him to stop. Her blood seemed to be sparkling in her veins. Her vision blurred, and when she at last bent her head to watch him take her, a new and stronger tremor started within.

She couldn't take her gaze off him. This man, this Marine, kneeling in front of her, holding her, exploring her body with his so-talented mouth. A groan built inside her and slowly escaped her throat. She gave herself over to the coiling tension tightening within. She felt as though she was about to spiral out of control. Her body hummed. Her brain spun, and still she strained to reach what was dangling just out of her grasp. Her hips rocked as she moved into him, wanting more, needing more.

Almost there. Instinctively she knew it and braced for whatever was coming. Calling out his name, Gina tightened her hold on his shoulders. Which kept her from falling off the edge of the world when the coil within her exploded suddenly, leaving her trembling and gasping for air that wouldn't come.

She swayed into him and, her body still pulsing, Nick stood and swept her up into his arms. Carrying her across the room in a few hurried strides, he stopped at the closed door and waited while she reached down to turn the knob. Walking into her bedroom, he laid her down on the bed, then stepped back to tear off the rest of his clothes.

Gina hardly had a moment to admire the hard, muscled strength of him before he was there, beside her, over her.

"I need you, Gina," he muttered.

She looked up into his clear blue eyes

and read the frenzied desire written there. She felt it, too. Even though she'd just experienced an actual earthshaking moment, the need was there again. Urgent. Desperate. "I need you, too," she whispered.

And in the next instant he pushed himself home.

She gasped, arching high off the bed even as she lifted her legs to lock them around his hips, holding him tightly inside her. Her mind worked to catalog this new sensation. This unbelievable feeling of having Nick Paretti *inside* her body.

Gina shifted, rocking her hips a bit, and he groaned tightly at the movement.

"Damn it, Gina," he murmured, looking down at her.

"What?" she asked. "What is it?"

He shook his head. "Nothing. Too late now, anyway." Then he bent to take her mouth in a kiss that rocked her to her soul. And after a long moment he moved his hips, sliding in and out of her warmth with a rhythm far more compelling than any piece of music.

Lost in the magic of it, Gina's hands skimmed over his back, up and down his spine, loving the feel of him pressed to her, reveling in the heavy, solid weight of him atop her.

In just seconds, though, the tightening began again. She felt it, and this time she knew what to expect, so she eagerly raced to meet it. Lifting her hips into his, she met him stroke for stroke, taking him inside her, deeper, deeper, until she wasn't sure where his body ended and hers began.

And just when she thought she couldn't bear the tension building within a moment longer, that glorious explosion overtook her again. She muffled a scream against his shoulder. Nick groaned ou her name as he gave one last hard thrust into her depths, and they held each other tightly as they soared and then slowly floated back to reality.

And the last Santini virgin bites the dust, Gina thought with a smile as Nick rolled to one side of her.

"This is perfect," he muttered, and threw his forearm across his eyes.

"Thanks," Gina said softly. "I thought so, too."

"That's not what I meant," he said, and levered himself up on one elbow to look down at her.

And such a look, she thought. All traces of passion and desire were gone from those incredibly blue eyes of his. Instead she saw a distrustful, wary gleam as he watched her.

"Well, what did you mean, then?" she

asked, disgusted that her happy little glow was fast disintegrating.

"Why didn't you tell me you were a virgin?" he demanded.

*That's* what this was about? For Pete's sake, what did her virginity or lack thereof have to do with him?

"Why would I?" she asked, meeting that accusing gaze of his squarely.

"Gee, I don't know," he said, and waved one hand in the air. "Because it would have been fair to warn me?"

"*Warn* you?" she repeated, as a flicker of anger erupted in the pit of her stomach. "I'm so sorry," she said, her tone letting him know that she wasn't sorry one damn bit. "I had no idea there were rules to be followed."

"Of course there are rules," he snapped. "There's rules to everything or there'd be chaos."

"I get it," Gina said, and rolled off the

edge of the bed. She thought better on her feet. "So you were expecting me to maybe wear a sign around my neck? Something in the nature of Watch for Falling Rocks? Or maybe Dangerous When Wet?"

When he only scowled at her, she continued.

"Oh! I know," she said, stomping to the closet and throwing the double doors wide. Gina snatched up the short, emerald-green silk robe hanging on the back of the door, slipped it on and turned to face him while she was knotting the belt. "How about—Virgin...Deflowering Required—would that have been enough?"

"Very funny," he muttered and got up, reaching for his pants.

"Oh, you want funny, *too.*" She shook her head and planted both fists on her hips. For goodness' sake, only a few minutes ago she'd been feeling downright fond of this man. Now she wished she were strong enough to pick him up and pitch him through the window. "You should really write down all the rules for me, Nick. That way we won't have any more mistakes."

"You should have told me," he said simply, shooting her an icy glance.

She would *not* feel guilty about this, she told herself. Every woman had the right to choose when and where and with whom she lost her virginity. She'd made the choice. Why should he have gotten a vote? It wasn't as though she'd asked him for a complete list of his previous lovers before they did the deed.

Ohhh! She thought. Good point.

"Why should I tell you I've never been with a man? You didn't tell me how many women you've been with."

"That's different," he snapped.

"How is that different?" she asked,

and threw both hands high in the air before letting them fall to her sides again.

He zipped and buttoned his jeans before answering her, and when he did, he looked directly into her eyes. "Because if I'd known, nothing would have happened here tonight."

"Then I'm glad I didn't tell." Because no matter how things were going now, the actual sex part of the evening had been spectacular.

She'd never expected to feel so much. To experience so many varied emotions and sensations. For a few brief, wonderful moments, she'd actually felt *connected* to this big ape. And damn it, he was trying to ruin the whole thing.

"Swell," he said, nodding his head as he reached down to snatch up his shoes and socks. "Then let me ask you this..."

"What?"

He paused for effect, then asked quietly, ''What happens when two people make love and don't take precautions?''

''Precautions,'' she repeated, then said the word again as reality started to worm its way through what was left of her happy little glow. A small curl of worry began to twist in the pit of her stomach. ''Oh.''

''Yeah, princess,'' Nick said. ''Oh.''

Gina folded her arms across her middle and held on tight. The one time in her life she'd gone with her feelings, given in to temptation and surrendered to what she was feeling. Oh, Lord, she wouldn't really go from virgin to pregnant in one easy step, would she? No. That couldn't happen, could it?

''I'd say we're lookin' at a real problem here,'' Nick said, ''unless of course, you happen to be taking the Pill.''

A lot of twenty-four-year-olds probably were on the Pill, she thought. But then, a lot of twenty-four-year-olds weren't virgins, either. She'd always thought that when the time came, she would be prepared. She'd know in advance. But nothing could have prepared her for tonight. Or Nick.

"And in a perfect world," Gina said, walking to her bed and dropping onto the edge of the mattress.

He sat down beside her, tugged on his socks, then shoved his feet into his shoes. After they were laced, he turned to look at her. "Whatever happens, we'll cross that bridge when we come to it. Pointless to worry until we know for sure, anyway."

She nodded. Sounded reasonable. And cold. And so distant, coming from a man who only moments before had been closer to her than anyone ever had before.

"How long till we know?"

"The longest three weeks of my life,"

she said, wondering if there was an extra cell or two in her body already. And what in heaven she would do about it if there were.

Three weeks to get to know him and three weeks to find out if they'd made a child together. Would the rest of her life be measured in three-week clumps?

"Okay." He stood up and looked down at her. "Three weeks it is. But no matter what happens, princess," he said, and waited until she was looking at him to continue. "I'm not marrying you. And you should know that right from the start."

Nick felt like a damned louse, but blast it, this was the only way. He wasn't going to be shotgunned into getting married. Especially because he'd been stupid enough and careless enough to bed a virgin. It didn't matter that making love to Gina had been the closest thing to a religious experience he'd had in years. It didn't matter that what he'd found in her arms was like nothing he'd ever known before.

He wouldn't be trapped or tricked or conned into getting married. Not again.

"Well who asked you to?" she said, and stood up to face him.

All right, maybe he should have phrased that a bit better. "No one," he said, "I just..."

"Wanted to ruin things a bit more completely?"

He heard a quick, rhythmic tapping and glanced down to see her right foot beating a fast pattern against the hardwood floor. Every inch of her compact body seemed to be quivering with anger.

"Forget it," he said, holding up both hands. "We'll talk about this another time."

"Don't look so worried, General," she

told him. "No one's dragging you to an altar."

"Look, I didn't want to start a fight, I just thought you should know how I feel about this."

"Well, thank you so much." She stood up and faced him, and Nick almost backed up from the rocket bursts flaring in her eyes. "I never asked you to marry me," she reminded him. "In fact, I just made a point of telling you I don't *want* to get married."

"That was before there was a chance you might be pregnant." There. He couldn't say it any plainer than that.

Clearly horrified, she drew her head back and sucked in a gulp of air. "You think—you're saying you think I—"

"What?"

Snarling at him, she planted both hands on his bare chest and shoved. As she pushed him backward through the doorway and into the living room, she kept right on talking. "You think I planned this? Hoping to get pregnant so you'd have to marry me?"

"I never said that." He tried to stop long enough to grab up his shirt and jacket, but Gina was on a mission now. And that mission was to get him out of her house.

She stopped only long enough to open the front door. Then she pushed him through it and onto the landing.

"That's what you're thinking, though, isn't it?" she snapped.

If he was, he sure as hell wouldn't admit it.

"You really are a Neanderthal, aren't you?" Glaring up at him. "This isn't the 1890's, you boob! A woman doesn't have to be married to have a child."

"No she doesn't," he said. "But it makes life a damn sight easier."

A cold winter wind whistled in off the ocean, and gooseflesh raced across his bare chest and back. A splash of water on his shoulder told him it was starting to rain, and Nick could only think that that would be the perfect ending to this little scene.

He hadn't meant to insult her. Just to warn her. Something she hadn't bothered to do for him. Damn it, if he'd known she was a virgin, he never would have slept with her. Virgins were too dangerous. They made too much out of something that was as natural as breathing.

Except, apparently, for this particular virgin. Wouldn't you know Gina would be as different in this as she was in every other way from any woman he'd ever known?

Gritting his teeth, he said simply, "Can I have my shirt and jacket?"

She glared at him and slammed the door.

It was as if the sound of that slamming door broke something in the sky. Because the clouds opened up, and rain sluiced down on him in a punishing torrent. A distant rumble of thunder only added to the dramatics.

He stared at the closed door for another minute or so, wondering if he should break it down and demand she talk to him again. An instant later that door opened up just long enough for his shirt and jacket to fly out and slap him in the face.

Then she was gone, and when he heard the lock click into place, Nick cursed under his breath and stomped downstairs.

# Seven

**O**ver the roar of the rain, Gina heard the pounding of Nick's feet on the stairs as he stomped off toward his car. She went up on her toes and peered out the peep-hole in the door, but she couldn't see any-thing beyond her porch.

Fine. She didn't really want to see him, anyway, she thought as she fought to slow down her racing heartbeat. Slapping one hand to her chest, she shook her hair back from her face and sucked one deep breath after another into her lungs. But it didn't help. She was still just as angry as she had been a few minutes ago.

Damn him, anyway! He'd practically accused her of setting a mantrap and then springing it on him. Well, even if she had been looking for a husband—which she was not—she wouldn't marry him. Not now.

"Heck," she muttered to the empty room, "I don't even want to *see* him again!"

But even as she said the words, she knew they weren't true. If you tell a lie and there's no one there to hear it, is it still a lie? she wondered.

Thankfully, the phone rang before she was forced to answer her own question. Hurrying across the room, she flopped down onto the couch, reached over and plucked the cordless phone from its cradle.

"Hello?" she said, and winced when she heard the grouchy tone of her voice.

"Gina?" A woman asked hesitantly.

"Yes."

"This is Cecelia Thornton..."

Gina's mind raced. Thornton, Thornton. Then she had it. The Colonel's wife she'd met in the parking lot after dance class. Good heavens, she'd forgotten all about their conversation.

"Is this a bad time?" Cecelia asked.

The absolute worst, she thought but didn't say. Because whether she was in the mood to deal with this now or not, it was just what she needed to take her mind off the Marine who'd just marched out of her life.

"Not at all," she lied, and forced a smile, to give her words meaning. Then, pushing thoughts of Nick Paretti to one side, she listened as the Colonel's wife talked.

* * *

Nick checked his wristwatch again, then looked out the front windows. The street was practically empty. Winter nights in an ocean town were too cold and too damp to attract many evening strollers. Wisps of gray trailed in from the sea, stretching ghostly fingers across the asphalt, and overhead, fog lamps dropped puddles of yellow light onto the parking lot. A small collection of cars sat waiting for their owners' return, and not one of them was Gina's.

Grumbling under his breath, he turned around again and let his gaze slide across the couples moving around the dance floor. Latin-flavored music swam through the room, and he told himself that since Gina had stood him up, at least he didn't have to try to cha-cha.

She could have shown up, he told himself, rubbing the back of his neck with one hand. This was not the Gina he'd come to know in the last three weeks. He'd fully expected her to be here, waiting for him, ready to pick up their argument from last night.

Instead, she'd left him standing alone like the wallflower nerd at a high school dance.

"Where's your partner tonight, Sergeant?"

Mrs. Stanton's voice came from close beside him, and he turned his head to look at her. Her blue eyes shone with interest, and a half smile curved her lips as she studied him.

"I don't know. Something must have come up." Like cowardice, he thought.

"Well," the woman said, lifting one hand to pat her hair that was sprayed as stiff as a football helmet, "there's no reason for you to miss a class simply because she has." Extending her hand toward him, she said, "I'll be your partner for the evening."

Oh, he didn't think so. He had enough problems already.

"Thank you, ma'am," he said, and didn't even notice her wince at the *ma'am.* "But I think I'll just drive over and check on Gina. Maybe she had car trouble or something."

And as he spoke, other possibilities occurred to him. Hell, maybe she was sick. Maybe she was too sore to move. He didn't know. He'd never been with a virgin before, and he hadn't exactly been gentle last night, he reminded himself.

Memories he'd been avoiding all day suddenly surged into his mind. Her touch, her sighs, her face as he pushed himself inside her. Along with the pleasure, he'd seen the flash of pain and discomfort dart across her features. Hell. As small as Gina was, he might have really hurt her.

"Damn it," he muttered thickly, and cursed himself for not having thought of this sooner. What if she'd been lying in bed all day in pain? Because of him? For all he knew, she was still lying there, trying to recover from what *he'd* done to her.

Wiping one hand across his face, he mumbled, "Excuse me," to Mrs. Stanton and headed for the door.

Nick parked his car on the street in front of the Santini house, got out and closed the door. He simply stood there for a minute or two, studying the old, craftsman-style bungalow, with its wide front porch and the welcoming patches of lamplight shining through the windows. A couple of houses down a dog barked, and from a distance he heard the solid slam of a basketball against a backboard.

A nice, quiet suburban street, where the

neighbors would keep tabs on each other and the world could slide by unnoticed. Nick shrugged deeper into his jacket and glanced at the sky. At least he wouldn't be rained on again. Stars glittered on a black sky, and the moon tossed shadows onto the street.

He started up the driveway, his shoes crunching on loose bits of gravel. An ocean breeze kicked up out of nowhere, pushing at him with icy fingers, then going on to rattle naked tree limbs like dice in a cup.

From inside the Santini house he heard the muted noise of the television set, snatches of voices and the sudden shout of a child's laughter. Gina's nephew, no doubt. As he neared the back porch, where he'd met Mrs. Santini only the night before, he glanced through the open curtains into the brightly lit kitchen and stopped dead.

Gina wasn't lying on a bed of pain.

So much for his theory about why she'd skipped dance class. Scowling to himself, he took a step closer to the house and stared right at her. She sat at the kitchen table, a bowl of ice cream in front of her, laughing at something the little boy across from her had said. Nick studied her for a long minute, not sure whether to be glad she was all right or mad that she'd stood him up. She wore a white sweatshirt, blue jeans and she had her dark, curly hair pulled into a short ponytail. She looked healthy, happy and too damned good.

And he'd been *worried* about her.

While, apparently, she hadn't given him a thought.

Small spurts of anger jumped into the pit of his stomach, and before he could think better of it, he was headed for the back door. He knocked loudly and rocked back and forth on his heels impatiently while he waited for her to answer.

Gina opened the door, still smiling at Jeremy. But when she saw who was standing there glowering at her, her smile dissolved instantly. All day she'd kept thoughts of Nick at bay. Anytime her mind drew up the image of his face, she'd countered it by remembering the way last night had ended. Remembering the anger, the hurt.

She'd even skipped the stupid dance class just so she could miss having to see Nick Paretti tonight. And what does he do? But she should have known. Nick wasn't the kind of man to be dismissed that easily.

"What are you doing here?" she asked.

"You missed class," he said.

Well, duh. "I didn't feel like going tonight."

"Why not?" he asked, folding his arms across his chest. "Chicken?"

Her gaze narrowed on him. "I am not chicken," she said, "though I have to say that sounds just a little juvenile, coming from one of 'The Few, The Proud, The Annoying.'"

"Damn it, Gina," he snarled, "I was worried about you."

She drew her head back and looked up at him. "Now why would you worry about me? You made it perfectly clear last night that you wanted nothing to do with me."

"All I said was, I didn't want to get married."

Gina kept her voice at a low pitch as she snapped, "And like I said, who asked you?"

He sighed, unfolded his arms and

reached out to grab hold of her, but she stepped back quickly. All she needed to shatter her weak defenses was his touch lighting up her insides like a fireworks display.

"Damn it, Gina," he grumbled, "we need to talk."

She shook her head. "Yeah, we were going to talk last night and look what happened."

"Who is it, Aunt Gina?" Jeremy asked from behind her.

She winced slightly and turned to look at the boy over her shoulder. Her nephew was watching her closely, and she knew that if she didn't get Nick out of there quick, the boy would be asking all kinds of questions and then running off to the den to report on what he'd observed to his mother and grandmother.

Forcing a smile she really didn't feel, she said, "He's a friend of mine. I just need to tell him something. I'll be back inside in a minute, kiddo.''

''Okay, but your ice cream's melting,'' he warned.

''You finish it for me, okay?''

''All right!''

Well, Jeremy's attentions had been diverted at least. Now all she had to do was contend with a certain Marine.

Stepping out onto the porch, she closed the door behind her and moved as far back from Nick as possible. Which, unfortunately, wasn't far at all, since the back porch was really nothing more than a wide top step.

''A friend?'' he asked, disbelief coloring his tone.

''What did you want me to tell him?'' she asked. ''That my lover of one night is here to start another fight?''

She heard his back teeth grind together.

''I didn't come here to fight,'' he said.

"I told you. When you didn't show up, I thought maybe something was wrong with you."

Besides bruised feelings? she thought. No, there was nothing wrong with her that having her head examined wouldn't cure. What had she been thinking last night? Then the answer to that question popped into her mind. She hadn't been thinking at all.

"Look, Nick, I'm sorry you were worried, but you can see I'm fine. So why don't you just go away?"

He shook his head, and she almost groaned at the stubborn expression on his face. Was he really that blind? That clueless? Couldn't he tell she didn't want to see him right now?

"Because we have to talk about what happened last night."

"Oh, no, we don't," she said. "Besides, there's nothing to say." She took the steps down to the driveway, where she wouldn't feel so hemmed in between his broad chest and the house.

He followed her down, and she backed up a step or two, not because she was nervous, but because despite the still-smoldering coals of her anger, just being near him was turning her bones to butter again.

Shoving one hand across the top of his head, Nick looked down at her and said, "You don't have to avoid me."

"Who's avoiding you?" she asked, and heard her voice crack, blast it.

"You are."

"No, I'm not," she argued, even though she knew she wasn't being very convincing. "I was just…tired, that's all. So I didn't show up for class."

She turned away from him and busied herself straightening out the car cover on Angela's new car. Her sister was so proud of the darn thing she did everything but sing it to sleep at night.

His hands came down on her shoulders, and he spun her around to face him. "That's not why you didn't show, and we both know it."

She squirmed out from under his touch before the warmth of his hands wormed its way into her bones. She did not need to start feeling warm fuzzies for this guy. It would be much safer to keep an angry distance between them. "It's really none of your business why I didn't show up."

"Lady," he argued tightly, "you *are* my business."

Okay, that got her attention. "Since when did I become your business?" she snapped.

"Since last night."

"Will you get over yourself?" Gina said, stomping away from him, farther down the driveway. She didn't want her mother and sister and Jeremy trotting out to find out what was going on. And she sure as heck wasn't going to invite him back into her apartment. So the safest place for them to talk would be out in the street. By his car. So he could leave immediately afterward.

The cold wind whipped past her, tossing her hair into her eyes and sending goose flesh racing up and down her spine. This was great. She'd probably get pneumonia. He was right behind her. She heard his footsteps slapping against the asphalt and hurried her own steps to keep ahead of him.

"Damn it, Gina," he said, and grabbed at her hand, dragging her to a stop at the end of the driveway. "Talk to me."

"You want me to talk?" she asked in a low hiss of sound. "Fine. I'll talk. You listen. I am *not* your business. You don't want a relationship? Well goody for you,'' she said, tipping her head back to glare up at him. ''Neither do I. And that includes having an overgrown Boy Scout as a personal bodyguard.''

He gave her a fierce scowl, and she got a brief glimpse of the professional soldier in him.

''I'm no Boy Scout, honey,'' he told her, his voice as low and furious as hers. ''And as for guarding that body, I wouldn't trust myself, because right now all I can think about is kissing you again, and that wouldn't get us anywhere.''

A flash of expectation roared through her, and Gina valiantly fought it down. Darn him, anyway. She didn't want to want him. But it seemed as if her body had ideas of its own. She sucked in a gulp of damp night air, hoping to put out the fires already beginning to build in her blood again. It didn't help. Best to just get him out of there, but quick.

She gave a look up and down the quiet street, grateful to see they were alone. On a cold winter night, most of her neighbors could be found sitting in front of either a fireplace or a television set.

"Listen up, General," she said as calmly as she could. "We had sex. That's all." Oh, brother, even she didn't believe that one. It had been more than sex. More than—she couldn't even come up with a halfway-decent comparison. But the main point to be made here was a simple one. "I didn't ask you to marry me. I didn't weep and wail at your feet, begging to be taken care of."

A muscle in his jaw started twitching.

"It was one night, Nick," she reminded him. "Not forever."

"One night that just might lead to a baby." He moved in close, actually *looming* over her.

"I'm not pregnant," she said, as firmly

as she could. Who knew? Positive thinking couldn't hurt.

"And you know this how?"

"I feel it," she insisted.

"Ah, so you're psychic."

"Psychic enough to know you're about to get kicked," she said, narrowing her eyes as she watched him.

"Look, Gina..."

Suddenly tired, she shook her head. "We're finished talking, Nick. Just go away," she said, and turned around, headed for the house again.

He stood there for a long minute, listening to the sounds of her tennis shoes on the asphalt. Then Nick grumbled under his breath and started after her. He caught up with her in a couple of steps and turned her toward him. Damn it, he'd come here to check on her and maybe to reassure himself that she wasn't counting on him to be a boyfriend or a husband.

He should be happy, blast it. He'd gotten exactly what he'd thought he wanted. He was in the clear. She couldn't make it more plain that she wasn't interested in him. Hell, she'd practically ordered him to leave.

So why was it that all he could think of was grabbing her and kissing her and doing everything they'd done the night before and then some? It didn't make sense. But then, nothing much had made sense to him since the night he'd met Gina Santini.

"You can't pretend it didn't happen," he said, looking directly into her eyes.

"I can if I try hard enough," she argued.

"No, you can't," he ground out. "Want to know how I know?"

She shook her head, but he told her, anyway.

"Because," he said, bending down until his face was just a breath away from hers. He inhaled her perfume and remembered the sensation of drowning in her scent, making it a part of him. "I've been trying to do just that all day. Want to know how well it worked?"

She shook her head again, and he kissed her. Kissed her hard and long and deep. Kissed her until his lungs were clamoring for air and his head was swimming and still he kissed her. He felt her surrender to him, and the moment she opened her mouth to him and he entered her warmth, he groaned at the sheer pleasure of the moment.

*This.* This is what he'd been needing all day.

His arms tightened around her, lifting her off the ground and holding her to him with a fierceness that staggered him. His hands fisted in the soft, fleecy feel of her sweatshirt. She wrapped her arms around his neck, lifted her legs and locked them around his hips.

Mouth to mouth, soul to soul, they clung to each other in the night. Neither of them wanted what they'd found together, yet neither of them could walk away, either.

His body throbbing, his blood pounding in his ears, he wanted to carry her back into her apartment and make love to her again. To find that exquisite moment of pleasure he'd known so briefly last night.

But in the next instant a door slammed across the street, and Gina jumped in his arms, tearing her mouth from his and staring at him blindly.

Her breathing as harsh and labored as his, Gina pushed free of his grasp and stood shakily on her own two feet.

Then she took one long step backward, lifting one hand to her mouth.

"Gina..."

"No." She shook her head and moved even farther back. "Go away, Nick," she said, and he heard the slight quaver in her voice. "Please go away."

# Eight

Gina wistfully glanced at the stairs leading to her apartment. But she couldn't go back to her own place. Not yet. She'd told Jeremy she would be right back, and she didn't want anyone in the house thinking something was wrong.

Because nothing was wrong. Right?

Nah, even she didn't believe that.

Despite the cold, damp air, Gina felt as though she was on fire from the inside out. From the tips of her toes to the roots of her hair, invisible flames licked at her. His fault, she told herself. He shouldn't have come here. Shouldn't have kissed her.

And oh, man, what a kiss, she thought, recalling the hard, solid feel of him pressed against her. The strength of his arms, the tension pounding through his body and into hers.

Her breath came in short gasps, and Gina slapped one hand to her heart. She was in some very deep trouble, here. Things looked grim when just *thinking* about a kiss could arouse her.

What she needed was time. Time to think. Time to kick herself for being such a wimp that the moment she saw him again, she was in his arms.

But what she had was an ice cream date with an eight-year-old.

Muttering under her breath about wishy-washy women and overbearing men, she opened the kitchen door and found not her nephew, but her older sister waiting for her.

"Where's Jeremy?" Gina asked, noting the two empty ice cream bowls still on the table.

"He's watching TV," Angela said as she picked up the bowls and carried them to the sink.

Okay, then, she didn't have to stay. She could go upstairs to her apartment and sit in the dark and think about what an idiot she was. Oh, goody. But she didn't even get to take a step toward the door when her sister's voice stopped her.

"So who's the hunk?"

Gina snapped a look at her sister and noticed the interested gleam in Angela's eyes.

"Hunk?" she stalled, shifting her gaze to a spot just above Angela's head.

"Real smooth, baby sister," the other

woman said with a shake of her head. Leaning back against the counter, Angela crossed her feet at the ankles, folded her arms over her chest and tipped her head to one side. "But one small suggestion. If you're going to pretend you weren't just lip locked with that guy, you might want to lose the bedazzled expression in your eyes."

"Oh, for Pete's sake," Gina grumbled, pulling out a chair and dropping into it. "Who are you, Sherlock Holmes?"

"Yeah," Angela agreed wryly. "It takes a real mastermind to look out a window and see your little sister climbing a man built like a mountain."

Oh, swell. This wasn't embarrassing or anything.

"You saw?" she asked unnecessarily.

"Enough to jump-start hormones I thought died two years ago." Angela gave up her casual pose and crossed the room to take a seat opposite Gina.

"How about Mama?" Ridiculous, she knew, to be twenty-four years old and worried that her mother had seen her kissing a man. But, there you go.

"Nope. Mama was too busy counting stitches in her new afghan to notice her youngest daughter scaling Mount Gorgeous."

Gina groaned.

"Come on," Angela coaxed. "Spill. And I want details."

Gina looked at her oldest sister and not for the first time, wondered why in the heck Angela had allowed herself to become such a hermit. Ever since her husband died, she'd acted as though she'd buried her heart along with the jerk who'd treated her and Jeremy so badly.

At twenty-eight, the eldest Santini daughter was tall and too thin. Her brown hair dusted her shoulders, and her dark brown eyes held a hint of sadness that Gina used to think would disappear with time. Now she wasn't so sure.

Angela had let herself slide into a rut so deep and so comfortable; she'd probably never leave it willingly.

On the other hand, while she was hiding here at home, she wasn't running into the kind of problems Gina had found. And speaking of problems…

"His name's Nick Paretti," she said finally.

"The dancing Marine?" Angela asked with a short laugh.

"The one and only."

Still smiling, her sister leaned toward her, resting her forearms on the tabletop. "But all you did was complain about him. Apparently there's been a change in attitude?"

She sighed. ‘‘Yeah, I know,’’ Gina said glumly. ‘‘Confusing, isn’t it?’’

‘‘You didn’t look confused when you were with him,’’ Angela said. ‘‘You seemed to know exactly what you wanted.’’

Did she ever, she thought. A new rush of heat swamped her, and Gina tried valiantly to tamp it down. But her blood still simmered and her body still tingled, so she gave up the fight and accepted the fact that Nick had an effect on her.

‘‘That’s the problem,’’ she admitted on a sigh. ‘‘I want him, I just don’t want him.’’

‘‘Well, sure,’’ Angela assured her. ‘‘Now I get it.’’

‘‘I didn’t say it made sense.’’

‘‘Good thing.’’

Well, nothing like having your big sister love and support you in your time of trial.

‘‘You know something, Angela,’’ Gina said, pushing up from the table, ‘‘it’s really easy to sit in a cave and tell everyone outside how to live. Why don’t you crawl on out and join the rest of us sometime?’’

‘‘What’s that supposed to mean?’’ Her sister asked, standing up to face her.

‘‘Just what you think it means,’’ Gina snapped. Even though a part of her knew that she was only yelling at Angela because she was furious with herself, Gina couldn’t seem to stop. ‘‘Your husband’s the one who died, honey. Not you.’’

Angela hissed in a breath as if she’d been slapped. ‘‘You don’t know anything about it. What it was like.’’

‘‘Your marriage? You’re right, I don’t. But I do know it’s over,’’ Gina countered.

The other woman looked furious enough to do battle, but all at once the fight died out of her expression and she shook her head. ‘‘You can’t understand,

Gina. Not until you're married yourself. Then you'll know what it's like to pin all of your hopes and dreams on one man, only to see them splintered."

Gina didn't think it was wise to pin your hopes and dreams on anyone but yourself. But then, she would never know, would she?

Gina sighed and shoved one hand through her tangled hair. "I'm sorry, Angela," she said quietly. "I didn't mean to yell at you. It's just..."

"It's okay." Her sister smiled. "Like I said, when you get married, you'll—"

"I'm not getting married."

"Well maybe not now," Angela conceded.

"Not ever."

Her sister smiled. "You can't know that."

"Yes, I can," Gina said, remembering a quiet night two long years ago and a whispered conversation with her father. And a vow she'd made that had changed the way her future would go.

"Gina?" Her sister's voice sounded different now. Concerned. "What is it?"

She shook her head. She'd never told any of them about the promise she'd made to Papa, and she wasn't going to start now. "Nothing. Look, uh, say good-night to Jeremy and Mama for me, will you?"

"Sure."

Gina turned for the door, and when she'd opened it, Angela's voice came again.

"Are you sure you're all right?"

She forced a smile she didn't feel and heard herself say, "I'm fine. Really."

Then she stepped into the darkness and closed the door behind her. Lifting her face to the star-sprinkled sky, she whispered, "If you're watching all this, Papa, I could use a little help."

"Did somebody shoot his dog?" A gasping, perspiring private whispered to the man running beside him.

"Hell, the dog probably shot itself just to get away from *him,*" the man countered.

The private chuckled until Nick came up behind him.

"Something funny here, Private?" he bellowed, never breaking stride, never slowing the rhythm of the run.

"No, Gunny," the Private yelled, gasping for breath.

"I don't have a dog, kid," Nick shouted, not the slightest bit out of breath, "but if I did, he'd be a Marine dog. Too tough to shoot, too mean to die. Just like me."

"Yes, Gunny," the private agreed, as loudly as he could, considering he was out of breath now and running on instinct alone.

"Now shut up and run before I get mad!" Nick called out.

The kid's eyes widened until Nick thought they might pop out of his head. But strangely enough it didn't make him feel any better at all to know that he still had the stuff to terrify Privates.

But then, nothing had made him feel better since leaving Gina's house two nights ago. He'd kept himself as busy as he could, yet thoughts of her still intruded, making his body ache and his head pound.

Even taking the platoon on a five-mile run hadn't helped clear his head. No, instead he'd found that he could run and think of Gina at the same time.

The thunder of dozens of feet pounding against the dirt track seemed to beat out a single phrase in his mind. *Call her, call her, call her.*

But what the hell good would that do? He wasn't looking for a permanent relationship, and nothing about Gina was temporary. So maybe it would be best all the way around if he did just what she wanted and stayed away from her. In three weeks he could give her a call and find out if God had a sense of humor or not and then they could go on their separate ways.

Yeah, he told himself, and gritted his back teeth. That's what he would do. Even if it killed him. Or the platoon.

"Double time," he shouted hoarsely, and ignored the chorus of groans lifting up from the tired troop as he picked up the speed of their run.

"Thanks for coming," Cecelia Thornton said, and poured Gina a glass of iced tea.

"Are you kidding," Gina said, "this'll be fun." She'd just spent the last hour going over details of the coming barbecue, and her head was bursting with ideas that would make this outdoor party a huge success.

"Thank Heaven you think so," Cecelia countered. "I'm just no good at this party-organizing thing."

"Hopefully," Gina replied, "lots of people will feel like that."

The night they'd met outside the dancing class, Gina had mentioned that she did party planning, and presto! Cecelia had snatched at the opportunity to avoid having to arrange her party alone.

Gina'd never bothered to mention the arrangement to Nick, and now she was glad she hadn't. Being here on base, she would no doubt have had to see him if he'd known she was coming. And she wasn't ready to see him again yet. The last two days had been hard enough.

She'd been living in a constant state of expectation. Always waiting for the phone to ring or to hear him knocking at her door. And when he'd done neither, she wasn't sure whether to be relieved or disappointed.

"So what do you think?" Cecelia asked, interrupting her train of thought.

Gina snatched her mind out of the clouds and forced herself to stick to thoughts of business. If she did a good job for Cecelia, maybe other Marine wives would want to hire her, too. She could be looking at the start of the business she'd wanted for so long.

"I've got a few ideas I'd like to talk to you about," she said with as much enthusiasm as she could muster. "Your patio is gorgeous, and I think with a few extra touches the party will be great.''

Cecelia grinned. ''I can't tell you what a relief it is to hear you say that. You know, I want to make a good impression.''

''That's natural, I guess,'' she said, taking a sip of tea.

''My husband thinks I worry about it too much,'' Cecelia said. ''But you know men.'' She sat up straight, wrinkled her forehead and deepened her voice. '''Throw meat on fire. Party good.'''

Gina laughed and relaxed for the first time in two days. She still felt a little guilty about being here under sort of false pretenses...after all, Cecelia did think that Nick was Gina's boyfriend. But after the barbecue they could have a pretend breakup and no one would be the wiser.

Yeah, she thought. This would work out just fine.

A knock at the front door made Cecelia smile. As she stood up from the table, she said, "I've got a surprise for you."

"Hmm?" A surprise? Gina watched her walk across the living room, and when the other woman opened the door, all the air in the room seemed to disappear.

"Mrs. Thornton, ma'am," Nick said, wondering why the Colonel's wife would ask him to drop by the house. Still tired from a lack of sleep and that five-mile run, he had planned to stop by the NCO club for a drink and then go home.

"Come in, Gunnery Sergeant," the woman said, and stepped aside, inviting him into the house with a sweep of her arm.

"Thank you, ma'am, I..." his voice trailed off as he spotted Gina, sitting at the Colonel's table. For one brief, horrifying moment, he wasn't sure if he was hallucinating or not. After all, why would Gina be here? On base? With the Colonel's wife?

But in the next instant he knew she was real. She looked far too dismayed to be a hallucination.

"Surprise," Cecelia said with a grin. "I thought you two might like the chance for a moment or two together, since Gina was on base, anyway."

Nick kept his gaze on the woman who'd been haunting him day and night. Rubbing one hand across the back of his neck, he tried to summon a smile, but the best he could manage was a baring of teeth. "Gina," he said. "What are you doing here?"

"She didn't tell you?" Cecelia interrupted, then turned to look at Gina. "I'm sorry. Did I spoil something? Were you planning on keeping this a surprise until the barbecue?''

''No,'' Gina said quickly, standing up and rushing to put Cecelia at ease. ''I must have forgotten, that's all. We've both been so busy.''

Busy, Nick thought grimly. Yeah, busy avoiding each other. For all the good it had done. He'd used every ounce of his willpower and self-control to keep from driving off base to see her—and suddenly, here she was. On his turf.

And looking as if she belonged there.

''Well,'' Cecelia said, looking from one to the other of them. ''Why don't you two go out and enjoy the sunset? I've got a couple of things to do in the kitchen before Jim gets home.''

''Yes, ma'am,'' Nick said, and moved across the room. He didn't wait for Gina to agree or disagree. He just took hold of her arm and dragged her along behind him as he headed for the brick patio beyond the sliding glass doors.

Once they were outside, he kept walking, not stopping until they were at the fence bordering the wide lawn. Far enough away from the house that they wouldn't be overheard, Nick asked, "What in the hell are you doing here?"

"Nice to see you, too, Sergeant Charm." She pulled her arm free of his grasp and started walking along the edge of the short wall.

He fell into step beside her. "Answer the question, Gina, what's going on?"

She shot a look at the house, then lifted her gaze to his. "Cecelia hired me to plan her barbecue."

"You plan barbecues for a living?"

"No. I work for a catering company now. But I'm starting my own business soon. Party planning." She lifted her chin defiantly as if waiting for him to make some sort of derisive remark.

Hell. Planning parties didn't sound like a fun job to him, but maybe that's because there wouldn't be any grenade tossing allowed. What did he know?

"Okay," he said slowly, "you plan parties. But how did you happen to end up here, planning the Colonel's party?"

"That night…when we met Cecelia outside dance class?"

He nodded, remembering it all too well.

Gina shrugged. "We talked, I gave her my number and she called."

Nick scowled to himself as he thought back. He did seem to recall the two women chatting while he was busy trying to find a way to keep his dancing lessons a secret. Man. He'd daydreamed for a couple of minutes and had missed all that?

"I thought you were a college student." He distinctly remembered hearing her say she had class on Friday nights.

"I am. But I also have a job. And a business I want to start." She glanced up at him and smiled too sweetly. "I'm a woman of many talents."

That's for sure, he thought, and wasn't even counting her jobs and school. She just kept surprising him. So much for his notion of her being the little princess. It sounded as though she put in as long a day as he did.

"Look," she said, coming to a stop and facing him. "I'm sorry if this is difficult for you, but I need this job. If Cecelia likes what I do, then maybe some of the other wives will offer me work, too."

More jobs on base? Oh, perfect. Now he could look forward to seeing her not only in his dreams but here, at Pendleton?

It was getting to the point where a Marine wasn't safe anywhere.

Still, looking down into her eyes, he could see how much this meant to her. And who the hell was he to try and stop her from making a living? He would only be stationed at Camp Pendleton for another eighteen months. How hard could it be?

Damn hard, he knew. He just wasn't sure if it would be more difficult to see her or to *not* see her.

"We don't necessarily have to run into each other," she pointed out. "It's a big base."

"One of the biggest," he agreed.

"So you don't have a problem with this?"

Oh, he had a problem all right. But it had nothing to do with whether or not she threw parties for Marines and their families. His problem stemmed from the fact that he was beginning to care too much about her. He thought about her too often. Looked forward to seeing her. Somehow or other, Gina Santini had crept past the defenses he'd erected across his heart. Now all he had to do was figure out if he was willing to let her the rest of the way in.

"I guess not," he said, and lifted one hand to smooth a stray lock of hair back from her eyes. Eyes that haunted him waking and sleeping.

She shivered as his fingertips slid across her temple.

"Nick..."

He let his hand drop to his side, and wondered where the hell all of his will-power was, now that he was standing right in front of her. He hadn't wanted to care for her. But blast if she hadn't made him care, anyway. "Damn it, Gina," he said tightly, ‘‘I miss you. I miss seeing you. Kissing you.’’

‘‘Don’t, okay?’’ she said, and backed up a step as if she didn’t trust herself to be too close to him.

But a moment later she looked up at him and admitted softly, ‘‘I miss seeing you, too.’’

Everything inside him went on full alert.

What had happened to all of his fine notions about keeping his distance? Right now all he could think about was getting her out of the Colonel’s backyard and to somewhere private where he could kiss her until neither one of them could draw a breath.

‘‘Gunnery Sergeant? Gina?’’ Cecelia called from the house. ‘‘The Colonel’s home, won’t you come inside and have a drink before you leave?’’

Gina's gaze shifted from his as she quickly started for the house. He thought he heard her whisper, "Saved by the bell."

# Nine

Gina kept busy. So busy she wouldn't have time to think. To remember. To want.

And it didn't help.

Her early-morning shift at the catering company crawled by while she helped to inventory a veritable mountain of supplies. Everything from tablecloths to silverware to champagne flutes had to be counted.

From there she stopped at a half dozen

party supply outlets and carefully picked through every kind of decoration known to man. From leis to stuffed gorillas to aluminum men from Mars, she saw it all, running from place to place, searching for just the right items to make Cecelia Thornton's barbecue a stellar success.

And when that was finished, she headed straight for school and the philosophy class she had no interest in attending.

Now she sat at the back of the class, half-asleep and trying to keep the grumbling of her stomach from drowning out the professor.

"Gina," the guy sitting next to her whispered.

She blinked, turned her head to look at him and forced a smile. Mike Gilhooley was a nice kid. But that's just how she thought of him. A kid. With his surfer-blond hair, pale-blue eyes and year-long tan, he looked every inch the California Babe.

Was it his fault she mentally compared him to a tall Marine with a no-nonsense military haircut and steely blue eyes? Heck, compared to Nick Santini, most men would come in a slow second.

"What?" she whispered, and winced when her stomach growled again. Heavens, she wished she was carrying a sandwich in her purse tonight. She hadn't eaten a thing all day, and she was as hungry as she was tired. Which was saying quite a bit.

Mike grinned and winked. "I thought maybe by the sounds of your stomach, I could talk you into going for a hamburger after class."

"Thanks," she said, tossing a glance toward the podium where the professor was outlining his lesson plan for the rest of the semester. "But I'm too tired. Think I'll just go home and crawl into bed."

Mike's blond eyebrows lifted, and he gave her his practiced smile. "Is that an invitation?"

"No," she said, shaking her head and smiling. He'd been trying to get her to go out with him for the past few weeks, and she just wasn't interested. Still, she gave him points for tenacity.

He shrugged good-naturedly and turned his attention back to the professor. Gina, too, looked straight ahead, but she wasn't listening. Instead, her mind wandered where it had been far too often lately.

Right to Nick.

Running into him at Cecelia's house yesterday hadn't been easy, but she'd better get used to it, she thought. If she intended to get more jobs out on Pendleton, then chances were she would be bumping into Nick once in a while.

Her eyes drifted closed as the professor's voice droned on and became nothing more than a monotone of white noise. Snatches of images and half-realized dreams drifted across her mind, and Gina slid deeper into the mist.

"Hey! Gina!" A shake on her arm brought her upright so quickly, she slammed her knee into the metal bracket of her desk and winced at the quick stab of pain.

Looking up at Mike, she blinked vaguely at his broad grin. "What are you doing?"

"Waking you up," he said, standing and hitching his full backpack onto his shoulder. "You've been asleep for the last half hour."

"Oh, great," she whispered, and gave a fast look around her at the emptying classroom. No one but Mike seemed to have noticed her little nap, for which she was grateful.

"No problem," he told her, smiling, "you didn't miss anything, anyway. Professor Johnson regaled us all with stories about his last trip to Nepal."

"Yippee...?" A nap sounded way better than that, even though she hadn't slept nearly long enough. Everything looked a little blurry and out of focus. She reached up and rubbed her eyes. They felt as dry as a couple of stones in a desert.

He laughed. "Exactly." Then he stopped smiling long enough to really look at her closely and ask, "Are you okay to drive home? I mean, I could give you a lift...."

One thing she didn't need was to encourage Mike in any way.

"No, I'm fine. Thanks, though." She

stood and gathered up her books and purse.

"You don't look fine," Mike said.

"Thanks again," she quipped, mentally forcing her tired muscles to deliver another smile. "Really. It's not far. I'll be okay."

"Okay..." He didn't look convinced.

With good reason, Gina told herself, since just the thought of having to walk all the way out to the parking lot was enough to make her want to lie down. But that was understandable since she'd hardly gotten more than a couple of hours sleep a night lately. And even those few hours had been restless...filled with images of Nick and the memory of his hands on her skin, his body filling hers, his kiss, his voice, his eyes.

Oh, God. How had this happened to a nice girl like her?

Before Mike could start in on her

again, Gina headed for the door. Concentrating, she managed to keep putting one foot in front of the other, focusing all of her will on first reaching her car and then home.

Nick stood in the grassy square outside the Humanities building. Leaning one shoulder against the trunk of a winter-bare tree, he kept his gaze locked on the main entrance, sparing only a brief glance at his wristwatch to make sure of the time.

Nearly ten o'clock. Her class should be over by now, he thought, letting his gaze drift slowly across the well-tended campus. Even this late at night, pools of light studded the walkways and grassy areas. But there were enough shadowy spots that the Marine in him rose to the surface, wanting to recon the whole place, making sure it was safe. Damn. This is just what he needed, thinking about Gina wandering through a dark campus out into a dark parking lot.

But even as he thought it, he knew Gina would call him a Neanderthal again and tell him in no uncertain terms that she was able to take care of herself. And maybe she was. But that didn't stop a man from worrying.

Hell. He didn't want to worry about Gina. He didn't want to care. Straightening up from the tree, he shoved his hands into his pockets and reminded himself again just why he'd come to meet her at school.

They needed to get a few things clear. They needed to set some boundaries. If he could, he would post an armed guard around his heart.

But since that was impossible, he'd come to the conclusion she'd been right. The only thing left for them to do—the only safe thing—was avoid each other. He would stop taking those damned lessons, first off. He'd learned enough to keep from hurling Majors' wives into punch bowls. And he would talk Gina out of that stupid contest idea, too. For her sake, of course. Why make it harder on her than it had to be.

The glass doors opposite him opened, and a few students trickled from the building and wandered out into the quad, their laughter and conversations sounding overly loud in the night. Right behind them came dozens of others, each of them hurrying out of class and on to the real business of a Friday night.

Something inside him quickened, and he refused to explore the sensation. He had a feeling he wouldn't like what he found. One or two of the girls glanced his way briefly, but Nick hardly noticed. He was too busy scanning the faces passing him, searching for the one face he wanted to see.

Anticipation pulsed within him. Almost like a kid on Christmas morning.

And then she was there suddenly, pushing through the doors, smiling up at a tall kid who looked as though he could pose for a Come to California Beaches ad.

Frowning to himself, he studied the pair of them. Nick's hands fisted in his pockets as he fought down an unfamiliar swell of jealousy. Hell, he used to laugh at the idiots who simmered and boiled because their women smiled at another guy. Now that the shoe was on the other foot, though, it wasn't comfortable.

He didn't much care for the way the blond guy hovered over Gina. And he wasn't real fond of the way she was smiling at him. It shouldn't matter to Nick, though, should it? Gina was a free agent, wasn't she? Damn it.

Stepping onto the sidewalk directly in front of them, he gave the beach boy a quick glare, then turned his gaze on Gina.

"Nick," she said, and even in the weird lighting he could see how tired she was. "What are you doing here?"

"Waiting for you," he said, letting his gaze shift meaningfully to the kid still standing too close to her. "We have to talk."

She shook her head and stepped around him. "I'm just too tired for our kind of 'talk' tonight."

She was kidding, right? He'd been standing out in front of her classroom for an hour and she was going to blow right past him? "Gina," he said.

"Is this guy bothering you?" the boy asked.

“Look, kid,” Nick started, though a part of him had to admire the guy’s guts.

Gina stepped in between the two of them and held up one hand to the blond beachcomber. “It’s all right, Mike,” she said quickly. “Nick’s a…friend.”

A *friend?*

“You sure?”

“Yeah,” Nick told him, irritation coloring his tone. “She’s sure.”

The kid didn’t look convinced, but he moved off, anyway. Ordinarily Nick might have given the younger man points for trying to protect a woman. Tonight, however, he wanted nothing to interfere with his conversation with Gina. Besides, if there was any protecting to be done, *he’d* do it.

As to the “friend” remark. Well, it was better than being an enemy, he supposed.

Once they were alone on the shadowy

path, the other students' voices a low rumble in the distance, Nick looked down at her and reached for her books.

She almost refused him, he could see it in her eyes, but apparently she was too tired to argue the point. She gave them over to him and started walking toward the parking lot. Nick fell into step beside her.

"How'd you know where to find me?" she asked.

"Stopped by your house. Talked to your sister."

"Angela."

"Yeah," he said, remembering the taller, thinner version of Gina he'd spoken to earlier. Angela might have made a great Marine. She'd given him a hard look and had him practically filling out a questionnaire before she would tell him where her sister was. Not a real trusting soul, but then again, why should she trust him? She didn't know him from Adam.

"Well," Gina said, and brought his attention back to her, "why are you here? Change your mind about not minding me doing parties on base?"

"No," he said, though it would be a helluva lot easier on him if she wasn't.

"Then what?" she asked, digging into that purse of hers and pulling out her key ring and the flashlight he'd seen before. Flicking it on, she turned the narrow beam onto the sprinkling of cars dotting the parking lot. Obviously, she'd done this a lot, since she seemed to have a pattern. First shining the light toward the closest cars, covering the ground around and behind them where someone might crouch in ambush.

Nick scowled to himself as he realized that she was used to doing this. It was second nature to her to watch for all possible places of attack. And though he was relieved to see she was careful, it bothered him more than he could say that she was out here alone most of the time.

But wasn't that what he'd come about? Wasn't he here to ensure that they went their separate ways? He didn't have the right to worry about what she'd be doing or if she was protected. He was trying to cut himself out of her life, so he'd better get used to the idea that he would never know if she was safe or not.

A twinge of something uncomfortable squeezed his heart. He could just see himself months from now, wondering about her—where she was, what she was doing. Who she was doing it with.

His back teeth ground together.

They reached her little compact car and she stopped at the driver's side door. Looking up at him, she yawned, covered her mouth with one hand and said, "Say what you came to say, Nick, because I need to go home and go to bed.''

Her stomach grumbled and she frowned.

''You also need to eat,'' he said.

''I need sleep more.''

She did look as though she was asleep on her feet. Maybe this wasn't the time for his talk, after all. It had waited this long, it could wait another day or two. Besides, taking care of her seemed more important at the moment. She was in no shape to drive a car. She could fall asleep at the wheel and wrap her car around a tree. His insides quailed at the thought.

''I'll drive you home,'' he said abruptly, and took her keys, pocketing them in his jeans. Then, taking her arm, he led her toward his car, parked a couple of rows over.

She tried to pull free, but she just

didn't have the energy. "And what about my car?"

"Leave it. You can come and get it in the morning. Have your sister drive you over." At his car he opened the passenger side door.

"No, I'm fine to drive," she said and swayed just a bit, giving the lie to her words.

"Yeah," he said with a nod. Head like a rock. "I can see that. Get in, Gina."

"God, you're bossy."

"I'm a Marine. Comes with the territory."

"Nope. You're a man. Comes with *that* territory."

He sighed. "Whatever. Just get in the damn car. *Please?*"

Pushing her hair back from her face, Gina sighed and surrendered. "I'm only doing this because I'm too tired to fight you on it."

"Hallelujah," he muttered, and slammed the door once she was in. He walked around to the driver's side, tossed her books onto the back seat and got in beside her. "Put your seat belt on."

Nodding, she grappled with the thing for a few minutes before Nick reached across her for the strap. His arm brushed her breasts, and she sucked in a gulp of air. He stilled for a long minute, then told himself to get a grip. Holding the belt, he pulled it across her chest and low over her abdomen then snapped it into place. She looked up at him, her face just a breath away from his.

"Thanks."

"For doing up the seat belt?" he whispered. "No problem."

"For driving me home," she said, and lifted one hand to touch his face, then reconsidered and let it fall back to her lap. "I guess I am too tired to drive."

"Yeah," he said softly, disappointed that she hadn't touched him. He craved the touch of her hand on him, despite knowing that he shouldn't. Just being this close to her stirred him in ways he'd never expected. Ways he wanted to deny but couldn't. "I know the feeling. Haven't been getting much sleep myself lately."

Her gaze filled him, softening in the dim glow from the parking lot lights. He read dreams and worry and confusion there, along with the stubbornness that had first attracted him to her.

"Silly, isn't it?" she asked, letting her head fall against the seat back.

"What?" Tearing his gaze from hers, he shifted in the seat, stuck the key in the ignition and started the engine. A low purr of well-oiled machinery rumbled into life.

"We started out enemies, became lovers and now we're—what?'' she asked, turning her head to look at him.

His eyebrows lifted. ''You told Joe College back there that we're...friends.''

''Bothered you, did it?'' she asked with a smile.

He muttered under his breath.

''What bothered you most, I wonder?'' she whispered, more to herself than to him. ''Seeing me with him or hearing me call you a friend?''

He shot her a look. Her eyes closed and she lay limply in the seat, a half smile on her face. Her deep, even breathing told him she was already asleep. Reaching out one hand, he caressed the line of her cheek and was ridiculously pleased when she turned her face into his touch, nuzzling his palm.

''To tell you the truth, princess,'' he said honestly, ''I don't know.''

Then he shoved the car into gear and drove out of the lot.

In a half-awake daze Gina felt him scoop her up into his arms. A night breeze ruffled her hair, and she cuddled closer to his broad chest, resting her head in the curve of his shoulder and neck. It felt good to be held by him again. Felt right to be cradled against his heart.

She kept her eyes closed as he started up the driveway toward her apartment stairs. She listened to the steady sound of his footsteps on the asphalt and knew she should tell him to put her down. But she didn't have the energy to fight him, and somehow she knew that she'd have to. He was clearly determined to see her safely home, and she was in no condition to argue.

Her own personal Knight in Marine Armor.

He took the stairs easily, as if her weight was inconsequential. She smiled into his chest. Every woman, whether she admitted it or not, had secret fantasies about their men carrying them off into the darkness. But not many men were strong enough to actually do it.

Their men. Oh, God. Is that what Nick was? *Her* man?

At the landing he took her keys out of his pocket, opened the front door and stepped inside. Closing it behind him again, he carried her to her bedroom and laid her down on the bed.

The soft mattress felt wonderful, and she instantly stretched and practically purred. Opening her eyes, she looked up at him.

He scrubbed one hand across his face as he watched her through hooded eyes. Seconds ticked by, and Gina felt caught by the strength of his gaze. A low curl of need started deep within her, and she tried futilely to keep it from spreading.

Nick Paretti had irritated, excited and infuriated her. But he'd also introduced her to real passion and made her wish that things could be different between them. More permanent. More—

"You'd better get some sleep," he said, shattering her thoughts. "I'll lock the door when I leave," he added, his gaze moving over her like a hungry man being denied a meal.

"No, don't," she said softly, reaching for his hand.

"Don't lock up?" he asked.

"Don't leave," she said simply, and curled her fingers around his, tugging him closer.

"Gina, we're both tired, and this isn't a good idea," he said tightly. She heard the strain in his voice and knew darn well that he didn't want to leave. He just thought he should.

"Then just hold me for a while," she said, wanting nothing more at the moment than to lie down beside him, cuddle in close and sleep dreamlessly for the first time in days.

Conflicting emotions darted across his face with lightning-like speed, until finally he nodded and eased himself down onto the bed beside her. Wrapping one arm around her, he pulled her close, nestled her head on his chest and whispered, "For a while."

# Ten

In her sleep she cuddled closer to the warmth of him. This was the best dream she'd had in days. Always before, Nick's image was ghostly, impossible to touch and yet enticingly real. But now it was as if her brain had finally gotten it right.

She ran the flat of her hand across his chest, and even through the fabric of his shirt she felt the strength of his hard, muscled body. Keeping her eyes tightly closed for fear of waking up and losing this moment, she molded her body to align with his, getting as close as she possibly could.

His arms encircled her, and she sighed at the warm, solid feel of him.

Gina moaned softly as tender hands explored her body.

In her dream, Nick lifted the hem of her T-shirt and slid his palm up, across her rib cage to the swell of her breast. His fingers tweaked her nipple through the lacy fabric of her bra and Gina sighed, moving into that dream-like touch.

This is what she'd wanted, needed for too long. Since their one night together, she'd hungered for more. Despite the fact that she knew they had no future—or maybe because of it—her need for him only seemed to grow stronger every day.

His hand slipped beneath the edge of her bra to touch her bare flesh, and when he did, her eyes flew open. The room was in absolute darkness but for the narrow slash of moonlight sliding through the gap in her curtains. It sliced through the shadows to lie like a laser beam lengthwise down the middle of her bed.

This was no dream.

Nick was here, with her. Where she wanted him.

She tilted her head back on his shoulder and met his gaze, and even in the dim light she saw fires burning brightly there.

Still fully clothed, they lay entwined together on her bed, and Gina wondered idly how many hours had passed. How much of the night was left. How much time they'd wasted in something as useless as sleep.

His fingers smoothed across her nipple again, and Gina gasped, arching into him. Swallowing hard, she asked, "How long have you been awake?"

"Since you threw your leg over me," he said softly.

She glanced down and noticed her right leg was still stretched across his body, as if even in her sleep she'd been trying to lay claim to him. Then she noticed something else. Beneath her leg, she felt his arousal, hard and ready, and her mouth went dry.

He wanted her as badly as she wanted him. He couldn't hide that from her, no matter what he might say in the next few minutes.

"Nick?" she whispered, shifting her gaze back to his.

"Yeah, princess?" His thumb and forefinger teased her nipple, sending hot, jagged bolts of awareness rocketing through her body right down to the soles of her feet.

"Oh..." Gina moved into his touch

again, as a wild tingling began building at her center.

She wasn't sure what she'd been about to say, and it didn't really matter at the moment, did it? Her mind whirling, her body humming, she pushed all thoughts aside and concentrated instead on what he was doing to her with a simple caress.

"Gina, honey," he whispered, rolling her onto her back and levering himself above her, "let me love you."

Her head cushioned by the mound of pillows beneath her head, she looked up at him and said softly, "Oh, yes. Yes, Nick. Please."

But the moment she agreed, his hand left her breast, and she wanted to cry out for the loss of it. His palm smoothed down her rib cage and across her stomach to the waistband of her jeans.

His gaze held hers as he quickly undid the button and zipper of the worn denim pants, making room for his hand to slide further along her abdomen.

Gina sighed and wriggled gently beneath him.

"Lift your shirt for me, honey," he said.

Keeping her gaze locked with his, she did what he asked, pulling the hem of her T-shirt up until her lace-covered breasts were exposed to his view. She shivered slightly in the cool night air, but the fire in his eyes warmed her an instant later.

"Now the bra," he told her, and Gina only nodded. Her breathing shallow and unsteady, she flicked the front clasp of her white lace bra and pulled it aside and out of his way.

He smiled at her, and she held her breath as he dipped his head toward her. Slowly he took first one nipple then the other into his mouth. Gina tipped her head back into the pillows and closed her eyes, the better to savor the feel of his mouth on her body. His lips and tongue worked over those two sensitive tips until she felt as though she might fly apart.

And while his mouth tortured her gently, his left hand stroked her abdomen, his fingertips just dusting the slim elastic band of her bikini panties. Gina's right hand fisted in her bedspread as she blindly searched for purchase in the world that seemed to be swaying around her. With her left hand, she held on to Nick, cupping the back of his head, holding him to her, keeping his attentions right where she wanted them.

He suckled her and as he did, he slid his left hand down, beneath her panties beyond the soft curls at the apex of her thighs, to the throbbing, pulsing heart of her.

She gasped and arched into him as he cupped her in his palm. He continued to draw and pull at her nipples, letting his mouth and tongue adore her while his talented fingers explored her soft flesh with tender thoroughness.

Her whole body felt taut, expectant. Gina lifted her hips into his hand, moving with him when he set the rhythm, clamoring for the release she knew awaited her. Again and again, he advanced and retreated, driving her ever higher and higher as her breath shuddered in her lungs.

Nick lifted his head and looked down at her. Eyes glazed, lips parted on a soft moan, she looked more beautiful than any woman he'd ever known. His heart thundering in his chest, a swell of emotion choked him as he bent to claim her mouth with a kiss.

He took her hungrily, his tongue mating with hers even as his fingers explored her. He felt her breath on his cheek, felt her arms wind around his neck, her hands clutching at his shoulders. Reluctantly he broke the kiss, pulling back far enough to watch her face. And then with one last brush of his thumb across the most sensitive part of her, he sent her tumbling off the edge of want into the safety net of contentment.

She called his name as the first explosion of sensation rocked her. He watched delight shatter her expression and felt the hard rush of it overwhelm him. And when the tremors slowly stilled, he rolled over onto his back, pulling her with him, cradling her to his chest. He stared up at the darkened ceiling and tried to understand what had just happened between them. For the first time in his life, Nick had been more concerned with pleasuring someone else than in taking pleasure himself.

Never before had he been satisfied to

simply give and do no taking at all. Yet now, though his body ached to join hers, it was enough to hold her. To know that he had given her something no other man ever had.

"Oh, my goodness," she said on a long, shaky breath.

He rubbed one hand up and down her spine, loving that she moved into him even closer.

"Good morning," he said, then smiled. "At least, I think it's morning."

She lifted her head off his chest, glanced at a clock on her nightstand, then lay back down again. "It's 3:00 a.m. That qualifies as morning, I think."

"Have to be at work in three hours, so, yeah, I guess it does."

"Nick," she said, and he looked down to meet her gaze. "That was…" She chuckled and shook her head. "I think I'm speechless."

He grinned, ridiculously pleased. "I must be good. Don't think I've ever seen you speechless before."

"Okay," she said. "I give you leave to be smug for a few minutes."

"Thanks."

"But what about you?" she asked. "I mean—"

He knew what she meant. And though he might regret it later, he heard himself say, "Don't worry about me. I'm fine."

"But—"

Nick sucked in a gulp of air, forcing his own needs into a tight dark corner of his soul. There was nothing to be done about it, anyway. "Gina," he said, "I'm fine, all right? Besides, I don't have any condoms with me and—"

She moved away from him and sat up, fastening the clasp of her bra and tugging her shirt down. "I may be new at this, but couldn't I do for you what you did for me?''

Instantly visions rushed into his mind, visions that did nothing to help him keep his rapidly disintegrating self-control in check. If she touched him, he knew it would never be enough. He'd want to make love to her completely, join their bodies. Sucking in a long, deep breath, he rolled off the bed and stood up. ''I'd better go.''

''Nick,'' she said, as she rebuttoned her jeans and scooted off the bed to face him.

Just looking at her, from her tousled hair to her just-kissed mouth, was enough to make him want to throw her down onto the bed. Hell, if she touched him, he'd be lost. He shook his head. ''Leave it alone, Gina.''

She actually flinched, and hurt flashed across her eyes as she stared at him for a long minute before nodding stiffly. He cursed under his breath as, a moment later, she marched across the room and hit the wall switch. Instantly bright light flooded the room, chasing away all of the dark, romantic shadows as thoroughly as though they were never there.

When she walked back and stopped directly in front of him, he saw the distant look in her eyes and mentally kicked himself. He'd managed to offend her, when all he'd been trying to do was protect her.

"All right, then. Why are you here, Nick? Why did you come to see me tonight?"

He reached for her, but she took a half step back. His hand dropped to his side. "I wanted to talk to you."

"About what?"

"About what you said the other night. That we shouldn't see each other anymore."

"Huh." A wry smile touched her mouth briefly as she glanced at the rumpled bedspread. "Not off to a very good start, are we?"

"That was my fault," he said, prepared to take responsibility for what had happened.

She raised her eyebrows as she just looked at him. "Let me tell you something, General. If I hadn't wanted that to happen, it wouldn't have happened."

"I know that, I'm just saying—"

"What exactly are you saying?" Gina snapped.

This was certainly going well. "I'm saying I think you were right before. We should avoid each other."

She snorted a laugh. "Oh, no problem," she told him and stomped past him, through the open doorway and into the living room. Still walking, she marched on into the kitchen and snatched open the refrigerator.

Right behind her, Nick watched as she rummaged angrily through her things before settling for a can of soda. She pulled it out, slammed the fridge door closed and flipped open the top of the can. Ignoring him, as only she could, Gina took a long drink, then slammed the soda onto the counter. Only then did she turn to face him.

"Are you still here?"

"Until we finish this, yes," he said, fighting past the tight knot of pain lodged in the center of his chest. Only a short while ago he'd been holding her, touching her, making her cry out in pleasure. Now she looked as if she was within inches of crying again. For a very different reason this time.

"Trust me on this. It's finished, Nick. Go away." She tried to push past him, but he grabbed her arm and held her in place.

"Not yet. Look, Gina, this isn't easy for me, either."

She slowly lifted her gaze to his.

"But it'll be better this way," he said. "We'll forget about that contest, and without the dance lessons, we'll only have to see each other at the Colonel's barbecue."

"Forget the contest?" she repeated.

"Yeah." At least one positive thing was happening here. She surely wouldn't want to keep dancing with him.

"No way."

He let her go and shoved both hands across the top of his head. "You can't be serious."

"You're darn right I'm serious," she countered, tilting her head back so she could glare at him full force. "The winners of that contest get five hundred dollars. And I can use that money. We're not quitting.''

''Oh, yes we are,'' he said.

''You coward.''

Nick stiffened as though he'd been shot. ''Nobody calls me a coward, lady.''

''What would you call it?'' she snapped, and this time did push past him to stride into the living room.

''Good sense?'' he asked, following after her into the shadow-filled room. ''Hell, I'm doing this for your sake.''

''Oh, that's a good one,'' she countered, whirling around to face him. ''How do you figure that?''

''Look at us, princess. The minute I touch you, we end up in bed.''

She laughed shortly. ''Trust me on this, too, Nick. I keep feeling the way I'm feeling right now and I won't have any trouble resisting your dubious charms.''

Damn it. Hardest-headed woman he'd ever met.

Gina was still talking, and he told himself to pay attention.

"Once we get through the barbecue, and the contest is over," she said, "*then* we can go our separate ways."

"Unless you're pregnant," he reminded her.

Gina quailed at the thought. She'd always wanted children. But not under these circumstances. Still, how hideous it was to be in the position of actually having to pray nightly that she wasn't carrying a baby. And even if she was…

"Whether I am or not won't matter. I'll handle it myself, I've already told you that."

"Yeah, that's what you say now, but sooner or later you'll want a father for that baby," he told her, moving in close enough that she could feel the waves of anger rippling from his body. ‘‘And trust me, honey. If you’re pregnant with my baby, you’re not going to be able to cut me out of your life.’’

She laughed, a harsh, tight sound that scraped her throat. ‘‘Cut you out? Heck,’’ she reminded him, ‘‘the first words out of your mouth after we made love were; ‘I won’t marry you.’’’

‘‘Who said anything about marriage?’’ he yelled, clearly as frustrated as she felt.

‘‘Not me,’’ she snapped. ‘‘I’m not getting married, remember? Not to you or anyone else.’’

‘‘Yeah, and why should I believe that?’’ he asked. ‘‘What makes you so all-fired different from any other woman?’’

‘‘Because I made a promise!’’ she shouted. ‘‘I promised my father on his deathbed that I would take care of my mother. Me. She’s my responsibility.’’

Oh, God. That was the first time she'd told anyone about what had passed between her father and herself the night he'd died. The night she'd given up thoughts of a family and realized that it would be up to her to provide for and protect her mother.

Silence dropped on the room. She heard the ticking of the wall clock marking off the seconds, and she waited, sure Nick would have something to say. She wasn't disappointed. Only surprised.

He laughed.

He actually laughed.

Shocked, Gina stared at him. After two years of keeping that secret locked inside her, she finally tells someone and he *laughs?* Beyond fury, Gina reacted instinctively. She slugged him in the stomach and winced as her small fist met incredibly hard, muscled flesh.

"It's not funny," she said furiously, shaking her stinging hand.

"Of course it is!" he said, throwing his hands high. "Are you nuts?" he asked. "Is this poor mother you have to protect the same woman I met the other night?"

All right, so Marianne Santini didn't seem like the kind of woman who needed taking care of. The point was, Gina had made a promise to her father, and she was going to keep it.

"You don't know her," she snapped. "You don't know my family. You don't know anything about us."

"Maybe not, but I know a strong woman when I see one," he countered. "What is she, fifty? Not exactly doddering. Besides," he went on, "you have two sisters. If your mother needs care, it should be up to the three of you."

Gina shook her head. He didn't get it. This was hers. Mama would need her, and she would be there for her. "No. Angela has Jeremy to worry about. Marie just got married. She'll be having her own family. It's up to me."

"Gina..." He moved in closer, his voice dropping as he reached for her. He wasn't laughing now. Understanding glimmered in his eyes, but she didn't want kindness from him. Not now.

"Don't," she said, hitching her shoulders and moving to one side.

"Okay," he said softly, "but let me ask you this. Do you really think your father meant for you to give up your own life? Your own future? Do you think that's what your mother would want?"

She'd asked herself those same questions countless times. But it didn't matter what the answers were. She'd given her word. She'd promised her father as he lay dying that she would look after Mama. And a husband and children of her own would only complicate matters. How could she devote herself to a husband and children, when taking care of Mama—keeping her promise—had to come first?

Besides, she couldn't ask a man to accept responsibility for her family. That was her job. Her duty. Her right.

"It doesn't matter," she said quietly as the storm of emotion passed, leaving her suddenly more tired than she'd been earlier. "I made a promise."

"I understand promises," Nick said softly, "and I keep my word, too. We'll stay in the contest, Gina. And we'll win."

She nodded.

He reached out and smoothed her hair back from her face before she could move away. Warmth skittered through her, and she looked up at him as he continued.

"Then, when we know one way or the other about the baby," he said gently, "we'll have another talk about promises."

# Eleven

The next week crawled by. Thoughts of Nick and their last real conversation plagued Gina almost constantly. Asleep, she dreamed about him. Awake, her mind refused to leave him.

She went through her days, trying to concentrate on reclaiming her life. Making it what it had been before Nick Paretti had marched into it. But then came the nights when they would meet for the dance class that had become a torturous experience. Being held by him, feeling his arms encircle her waist, his body press close to hers while all around them music swelled was far more difficult than she'd told herself it would be.

But she wouldn't quit. She wouldn't let him know that he'd been right. That spending three nights a week in his arms and the rest of the time away from him was becoming unbearable. In fact, her only consolation in all this was the sure knowledge that he was having as hard a time dealing with the situation as she was. She felt it in his touch. In the way he tried to hold her impersonally even while his gaze melted her bones.

Darn him, anyway, for confusing things. For two years she'd been resigned to a future that didn't include a family of her own. She'd made a vow to her father and had accepted what that vow would cost her. She'd made peace with it. Now

Nick Paretti storms into her life and throws a monkey wrench into everything.

*Do you think your father meant for you to give up your own life? Is that what your mother would want?*

The echo of Nick's voice pounded through her head. As she listened to those questions reverberating over and over again, Gina had to admit she still didn't have an answer. Why did he have to make this all so hard?

"Okay," she said abruptly as she deliberately tucked thoughts of Nick into the deepest corner of her mind, "that's enough. No more thinking. You have a barbecue party to throw, and it had better be a good one if you want anyone else to hire you."

She didn't even want to think about how lonely her voice sounded in the apartment and how she would probably spend the rest of her life talking to herself—because she wouldn't have anyone else. She wouldn't have Nick.

Once this barbecue and the dance contest were over, they'd go their separate ways. An ache settled around her heart, and she wondered sadly if it would be with her forever.

"Didn't Gina do a lovely job," Cecelia Thornton said, loudly enough to be heard above the muted roar of conversations rising around them.

Nick smiled and let his gaze sweep across the crowded scene.

Cobalt blue glasses in varying heights sat on the tables sprinkled around the backyard and across the brick patio. In the half-light of dusk the lit votive candles inside the glasses sent flickering points of blue flame sparkling around the yard. Red-and-white-checked tablecloths looked fresh and summery in the middle of winter and the navy-blue plastic dinnerware completed the patriotic theme. Red and white carnations in blue-and-white spatterware jugs adorned every table and an old-fashioned juke-box rented for the occasion sent big-band music from the forties drifting across the yard.

"Yes, ma'am," Nick agreed, feeling a flash of pride in Gina's accomplishment, "she really did."

"It's just what I wanted," the woman went on as she had been doing for the last five minutes. "An old-fashioned picnic, informal but stylish. And it's turned out beautifully. Even the weather cooperated."

It had been a nice day, and now that the party was nearly over, Marines and their spouses milled around the backyard, talking and laughing. A few couples danced to the music floating out of the juke-box while others stood on the sidelines offering critiques. The scent of grilled steaks still hung in the air, and if he hadn't known better, Nick would have sworn it was summer.

But if it were summer, then Gina wouldn't have been here, pretending to be his girlfriend. She would be out of his life, and they would have already drifted apart. Strange how the thought of that opened up a dark hole inside him. His gaze shifted to the last place he'd seen her. She was still there, standing in the middle of a group of wives, laughing and talking as though she belonged. As though she were a part of this scene and not just playing a role.

A knot formed in his chest and tightened, threatening to close off his breath. Damn it, he wished it were real. He wished he and Gina really did have what they were only pretending to have. His gaze dropped to her flat abdomen, and for the first time he found himself almost hoping she was pregnant.

"Well," Cecelia said, her gaze following his, "enjoy yourself, Gunnery Sergeant."

"Yes, ma'am," he muttered dutifully, still stunned at the flood of new realizations swamping him. "I will."

She moved off, and Nick hardly noticed she'd gone. All he could see was Gina. All he could think about was Gina. But since the night she'd told him about the promise she'd made to her father, Gina had never been far from his mind.

How could he have thought she was like his ex-wife? Kim wouldn't have given up a day of *shopping* for someone else, let alone her future. He admired Gina's ferocious loyalty toward her family. Hell, there was plenty he admired about Gina. Plenty he would miss.

That thought brought him up short.

Scowling to himself, he moved off toward the knee-high wall surrounding the Colonel's yard. Away from the people, distanced from the music and the conversations, Nick rubbed the back of his neck viciously and told himself it didn't matter. He'd never intended to be a part of Gina's life. To be with her forever. He'd known from the beginning—from the first moment he'd seen her at that damned dance class, that this would be a temporary thing.

So why was it so hard now to acknowledge that their time together was almost over? Because, he told himself, he hadn't counted on loving her. *Love?*

"Hey, Gunny," a deep, familiar voice shook Nick from his thoughts, and he reluctantly looked away from Gina to face the man walking toward him.

"Hi."

First Sergeant Dan Mahoney stopped

alongside him, took a drink of his beer, then used the long-necked bottle to point across the yard at Gina. "Pretty woman."

Nick shot his friend a suspicious glance. The man had a hell of a reputation with women. "Yeah? What's your point?"

Dan shrugged good-naturedly. "The point is, are you two an item or not?"

A good question. One he didn't have an answer to. "What do you think?"

"I think you're supposed to be here together, but I don't see you together much."

"So?"

"So," Dan said, "if you're not interested in her..."

"Who said I wasn't interested?" Nick straightened up and glared at his friend.

"So why are you here with me when you could be over there with her?"

A long minute ticked by as Dan's

words sank in. Finally Nick laughed shortly. He had so little time left with her, and instead of being with her every minute, he was sitting here sulking and wishing things were different. Well, the only way things would be different is if he *made* them different. "You're right, damn it." Nodding to himself, he glanced at Gina. He hadn't planned on caring for her. Hadn't wanted to find love again. But now that he had, was he willing to let it disappear?

Mind racing, Nick started across the yard toward her. As if she sensed him coming, she turned, and their gazes locked as he neared her. Staring into her brown eyes, Nick saw her warmth, her spirit, the laughter he'd come to expect from her. She smiled and his heartbeat staggered. How could he have thought he could live without her?

* * *

The voices of the women around her faded into nothingness as Gina stared into Nick's blue eyes. What was he thinking? What was he feeling? And more important, how could he set fire to her blood just by looking at her? A twist of anticipation coiled in the pit of her stomach and tightened as he came closer. All afternoon she'd pretended to be a bigger part of his life than she was. She'd listened to the stories from the other men's wives, felt the strong sense of kinship they shared and wished she were a part of it. She'd watched Nick in his element, and even here, surrounded by professional warriors, he seemed to stand out from the rest.

And watching the obvious respect with which he was treated, she'd felt proud to be with him.

Gina held her breath as he stepped up to the small knot of women, his gaze still boring into hers. His dark-blue sports shirt seemed to make his eyes even bluer than usual. Then he spoke, and the rumble of his voice trembled along her spine, making her knees weak.

"Ladies," he said, nodding, "if you don't mind, I'd like to steal my girl away."

His girl. Pleasure simmered inside her. She knew he was only saying that to keep up their pretense. But somehow she found herself wishing he meant it.

"I don't know, Gunny," one of the women said, "we kinda like her."

He spared the woman a smile and said, "So do I." Then he reached for her hand, and electricity seemed to shimmer up from her fingertips, along her arm to the center of her chest, where it lit up her heart like lightning in a summer storm. His hand closed around hers, and he squeezed tight as he led her away from the crowd to a relatively private corner of the yard.

"You did a good job today, Gina," he said softly, pulling her closer.

"Thank you," she said, tipping her head back to look up at him. Gina swallowed hard as she felt his right hand slide around her waist. A cool breeze ruffled her hair and teased at the collar of her blouse. But she wasn't cold. How could she be, with the fire in Nick's eyes to keep her warm?

"Party's about over," he said, his voice as deep and dark as a restless dream.

"Uh-huh," she whispered, concentrating on the feel of his fingertips against her back. Even through the silky fabric of her blouse, she felt the warmth of him seeping down deep inside her. Her stomach flip-flopped. Her breath hitched in her lungs.

He lifted his head briefly to look about the yard, then shifted his gaze back to her. She lifted one hand to touch his cheek, and she watched the muscle in his jaw twitch as he gritted his teeth. Knowing she had such an effect on him only heightened the tensions running through her.

"I want to see you," he said quietly, hungrily, "away from this crowd. Alone."

She knew exactly what he meant, and instantly her own body went on full alert. It was as if she'd been keeping these feelings at bay all week and now suddenly they'd broken free. Need rippled through her, and Gina didn't want to question it. "Me, too."

"Come on, then," he said suddenly, grabbing her hand and holding on tightly. He led her through the crowd, and Gina saw all of the faces she passed as little more than a blur. Body humming, she hurried alongside him and muttered polite phrases as they said goodbye to the Colonel and his wife.

Then Nick and Gina headed toward the front of the house. "Where'd you park your car?" he asked tightly.

"There," she said, pointing. He nodded and started for it. "What about yours?" she asked.

"I walked. Only live a few blocks from here."

"That's close," she said.

"Real close," he agreed, giving her a look that nearly set fire to her soul.

"Oh, good," she muttered, and only let go of his hand long enough to give him her keys, then get in on the passenger side. "You drive. It'll be faster."

"Yeah." Jaw tight, he stared straight ahead, as if he didn't dare look at her for fear of wrapping the car around a lamppost. But he stretched his right hand across the space separating them and ran his palm up and down her thigh.

"Oh, hurry, Nick," Gina whispered, lifting her hips right off the seat to move into his touch. When his hand dipped down, between her thighs, she groaned tightly and managed to say, "Please tell me you have condoms."

"Oh, yeah," he muttered, stroking the hot, aching center of her through the tight denim fabric of her jeans.

"Oh, good."

In seconds they were pulling up in front of a long row of apartments. Gina didn't even bother to look around. She wouldn't have seen anything, anyway, through the hazy blur masking her vision. He jumped out of the car, came around and opened her door for her, then pulled her out of her seat with one strong tug. Keeping a tight grip on her hand, he led her to one of the doors on the ground floor and fumbled in his pants pocket for the key.

When he had the door opened, he guided her inside, then closed and locked the door behind them. Gina turned and flew into his arms. This, she told herself as his hands swept up and down her back, cupping her behind, stroking her spine, this is what she wanted. Needed. This man. This wild, amazing loving.

He kissed her, opening her mouth with his tongue, demanding her response, and when she gave it, he groaned and tightened his hold on her. Again and again, their tongues twisted together as he walked her through the apartment. Breath mingling, souls touching, his hands explored her even as his mouth devoured her.

When the backs of her knees came up against the edge of his bed, they stopped, and frenzied hands went to work on buttons and zippers. In seconds they were naked, wrapped together atop the quilt.

His hands were everywhere. Gina's mind raced to keep up with the sensations pouring through her, and still she was breathless. Her palms slid up and down his back, and she marveled at the solid strength of him. The feel of his weight pressing into her, the scent of him filling her, the taste of him on her mouth. All these things she would remember. She imprinted them all on her memory, wanting to be able to recall every moment spent with him. Every touch. Every kiss.

He touched her center, and she was ready for him. Damp heat welcomed him, and she gasped as she lifted her hips into his touch. Closing her eyes, she muttered, "Oh, Nick, please..."

"Just a minute, baby," he whispered, and leaned away from her. She heard a drawer slide open and then a tearing sound and she knew he'd sheathed himself.

Opening her eyes again, she watched as he came back to her, moving to kneel between her legs, sliding his palms up the insides of her thighs until she trembled from the want building within her.

"Be inside me, Nick," she whispered, lifting both arms toward him.

"That's right where I want to be, Gina," he said softly, and covered her body with his own.

He took her mouth with his in a glorious invasion. She met him kiss for kiss, sigh for sigh and held him tightly as he set a hard, fast rhythm that sweetly tortured her. As tension within her mounted, she smoothed her hands up and down his back, her short, trim nails tearing at his skin as she struggled to find something to hold on to in a suddenly tilting world.

Bodies as one, hearts pounding, they hurtled toward the peace they'd only found together. And when Gina arched into him and cried out his name, Nick knew he could never give her up.

A few minutes later Nick snatched Gina's blouse off the floor and handed it to her.

"Thanks." She slipped it on and began to button it.

"Gina," he said softly, as he tugged on his jeans, "I've been thinking."

She threw him a quick look, then grabbed up her khaki slacks. "About..."

"Us," he said simply. "This." He waved one hand at the rumpled bed cover. "What we have together."

"Nick..."

"I think we should get married."

"What?" She stopped, her hands still

gripping the snap at the waistband of her slacks.

He shoved one hand across the top of his head and paced barefoot around the room. Nice job, Paretti, he told himself. Real smooth. Hell, *he* hadn't expected that to come flying out of his mouth any more than she had.

Shaking her head, she backed away from him. "Oh, why'd you have to say that?" she asked, and he heard the slight tremor in her voice.

He laughed shortly. "Surprised the hell out of me, too."

"Don't do this to me, Nick," she said softly.

"I'm not trying to *do* anything to you."

"I can't marry you," she reminded him, and tossed her hair back out of her eyes. "I made a promise."

"A promise no father would want to

hold his daughter to,'' he said, knowing it was the truth.

''I gave my word. Besides, you're probably proposing for no reason.'' A glimmer of tears shone in her eyes before she blinked them back.

He knew exactly what she meant, and it rocked him to his heels. ''You think I'm proposing because you *might* be pregnant?''

''Why else?'' she snapped, and a single tear rolled unheeded down her cheek. ''You've already said you never wanted to get married again.''

''I changed my mind,'' he shouted.

''Well I didn't,'' she shouted right back.

''Look, Gina,'' he said, trying to get things straight in his mind, ''I admit, I never wanted to get married again. But we have…something together. Something I never expected to find.''

"People don't get married because they had sex," she told him, swiping at that tear with the back of her hand. "At least not in this century."

"It's more than that, and you know it."

"No," she said, shaking her head and biting down hard on her bottom lip. "I won't let it be."

"You want to take care of your mother," he said, moving toward her. "I can understand that. I can help."

She shook her head again. "I don't need your help. Where are my shoes?"

"I didn't say you needed it," he countered, while she searched the floor. "I'm just saying—"

"I know what you're saying," she interrupted, and stepped into one of her black loafers, "but I don't need your family money to take care of my mother."

"Damn it, Gina," he said, frustration

coloring his tone, "I'm not talking about my family money. I'm talking about me."

Her gaze slid from his. "Where's my other shoe?"

"The hell with your shoe," he snapped. "What about us?"

"There is no us," she said, and her breath hitched on a choked-off sob. "Oh, the heck with this, I don't need the other shoe."

Then she started for the front door, one shoe on, one shoe off, her footsteps making an odd sound on the floor as she went.

Everything in him went cold and still. If he didn't think of a way around this, he thought, she would keep walking, right out of his life.

"Gina," he said as he caught up with her and grabbed hold of her arm, turning her around to face him, "if you're pregnant, you *will* marry me."

Gina looked up into his eyes, lifted one hand to his cheek and said, ‘‘Goodbye, Nick.’’

And damned if it didn’t sound permanent.

## Twelve

"Where's your other shoe?"

Gina stopped dead and glanced at her mother, seated on the back porch steps. She'd hoped to sneak past the house and into her apartment where she could lick her wounds in private. Of course, the way her day had gone, she should have known better.

"I, uh...lost it."

In the glow of the porch light, she saw one of her mother's eyebrows lift. "Must have been a good party."

She nodded and started walking again.

"Where's your boyfriend?" her mother asked as Gina came even with her.

"He's not my—" She stopped herself and shook her head.

"Ah," Marianne said sagely, "you had a fight."

Gina looked at her mother and was nearly swamped by the urge to crawl into her lap. Strange how quickly a grown woman can become a child again around her parent, she thought.

"What did he do wrong?" her mother asked gently.

"He asked me to marry him."

"He moves fast." Mama grinned. "And this was worth fighting about?"

"I said no." Gina closed her eyes tightly against the memory of his face as she'd left him. But even if she'd been free to marry him, she wouldn't have. He'd never said anything about love. How could she say yes to a hurried proposal for the sake of a baby? What kind of marriage would they have if forced together for convention's sake? What kind of life would it be for the child?

"Sit down." Mama said and grabbed one of her hands to tug her over to the porch.

From within the house came the ordinary sounds of a typical evening—Angela and her son arguing over doing the dishes, with the rumbled noise of the television in the background. And at the far end of the street, Mrs. Harkin's poodle yapped at nothing as the streetlights blinked on. Everything was so ordinary and yet…so different. Gina took a seat beside her mother on the cold, cement step and leaned against her.

"Tell me why you said no."

"I had to."

"Do you love him?"

"Yes," Gina whispered, and realized it was the first time she'd acknowledged her love for Nick, even to herself. He was everything she could have asked for—strong, kind, stubborn, passionate.... Oh, yes, she loved him. But that changed nothing. "And I can't marry him."

"You're not making sense."

Gina sat up straight and turned her head to look at her mother. How to explain? "I—"

Her mother's eyes narrowed suspiciously. "What?"

Gina sighed. "I never meant for you to know."

"Well now I *have* to." She gave her daughter a look Gina hadn't seen since childhood. "Talk."

Gina surrendered—maybe because she needed to—and in just a few short minutes, she'd told Mama everything. Silence stretched out between them for several long minutes, and then her mother grumbled something and jumped to her feet.

"Take care of me?" she asked, tilting her head back to look up at the darkening night sky with an accusatory scowl. "You asked our daughter to take care of me?"

"Mama..."

Muttering in Italian, Marianne Santini spun around to face her daughter. "Gina, honey, I loved your father very much, but sometimes..."

Confused, she asked, "What?"

"Think about it, honey. Who was it who took care of the bills, did the bookkeeping, watched you girls, managed the house and the shop?"

She didn't have to think about it. "You did."

"Uh-huh," her mother said, planting

both hands on her hips. ‘‘I didn’t need your papa to take care of me,’’ she said. ‘‘I needed him to love me.’’

‘‘He did.’’

‘‘Yes, he did.’’ She reached out to cup Gina’s cheek. ‘‘But my point here is, I can take care of myself.’’

‘‘But Papa…’’

‘‘Papa was wrong,’’ her mother said, interrupting her firmly and shooting another scorching glare skyward before looking at her daughter again. ‘‘I love you, honey,’’ she said, ‘‘but I don’t need a nurse. What I need is for you to be happy.’’

Nick had been right. Marianne Santini was an amazing woman. Gina stood up and walked right into the circle of her mother’s arms. Where she’d always felt safe. Loved. After giving Gina a fierce hug, her mother took her by the shoulders and looked deep into her eyes. ‘‘You be happy, Gina. Married or single, whatever it is you want. I'll support you. Always."

"I know that, Mama."

"Good. Now, you forget about that promise, because when I talk to your papa tonight, I'm going to give him a piece of my mind."

Gina grinned through the tears blurring her vision. She didn't envy her father. Even being in Heaven didn't get him out of reach of Mama's temper.

"Now!" the other woman said briskly, "you go upstairs and wash your face. Maybe call that nice boy. Straighten this out. Me, I have to get ready for my date."

Gina's jaw dropped as she watched her mother take the back steps. "You have a date?"

"Hmph! What? I'm so terrible a man wouldn't want to date me?" Her mother smiled. "Like I said, I can take care of myself. Now it's time for you to do the same."

Alone in the darkness, Gina realized that her mother, far from needing a protector, had a much firmer grip on her life than she did. But she had always known that, deep down. Maybe she'd been hiding behind that promise to Papa. And, free of her promise, Gina was still unable to have the man she wanted, because he was only interested in protecting a child that might not even exist.

One week later Nick stood just inside the hall where the dance contest was being held. Keeping one eye on the front door and a wary eye on the panel of judges opposite him, he tried to tell himself it would work out. It had to work out.

He'd tried all week to talk to Gina, but she'd avoided him with a stealthy dexterity that should have earned her a position in the Recon Battalion. His last chance at talking to her, reasoning with her, was this stupid contest. And for that chance he was even willing to humiliate himself in public.

Man, he'd be a lot more confident right now if he was wearing fatigues and carrying an M-16.

Then the front door swung open, and suddenly Gina was there. Pausing in a pool of lamplight, she glanced around the crowded room until she saw him. Her hair curled in gentle waves and was pulled back from her face by a rhinestone clip that glittered in the overhead light. She wore a soft-green dress with a neckline low enough to tantalize him and a full skirt that swirled around her knees as she came toward him. She looked beautiful, he thought, despite the gleam of sadness in her eyes that hit him low and hard.

* * *

One look at him and Gina knew she probably shouldn't have come. Lord knew she'd long since stopped caring about this darn contest. But at the same time, this was her one last chance to see him—to talk to him. And she had to tell him; he had the right to know. Then he could go on with his life, and she could start learning to get over him.

But it wouldn't be easy. Her heart fluttered unsteadily as her gaze swept over the handsome figure he made in his dark-brown sports jacket and khaki slacks. But it was those blue eyes of his that did her in. As they had from the first moment she'd seen him.

A swell of music rose up in the air, and contestants and audience members alike drifted toward the huge dance floor, leaving the two of them alone in the entryway.

"You're late," he said.

"Yeah, I know," she answered. Actually, she'd been on time, she'd just spent a few extra minutes in the parking lot, steeling herself to go inside.

"Gina—"

"Before you say anything," she said quickly, wanting to stop him before he did something stupid like propose again, "there's something you have to know."

"All right."

It shouldn't be this hard, she thought, staring into his eyes. She should be happy. She should be relieved. Instead, she felt like crying.

"There's no baby." Gina said the words in a rush, hoping to get them out before her voice broke. God's little "all clear" signal had arrived that morning, and she'd been sorry about it ever since. Now not only wouldn't she have Nick, she wouldn't have his child, either. Logically she knew it was better this way.

Unfortunately, logic didn't have much to do with her feelings.

A long, silent moment drifted by as he only looked at her blankly. Then he asked, "Are you sure?"

Gina choked out a humorless laugh. "Yes, I'm sure."

"Yeah," he muttered, running one hand across the top of his head. "Of course you are. It's just…"

She couldn't tell what he was thinking, and maybe that was just as well. She didn't want to see his relief. His delight in the narrow escape he'd just had. And she didn't want to stand in this cold, empty vestibule talking about how *lucky* they were, either.

Lifting her chin, she started past him, toward the dance floor. She would do her part in this contest and then she'd go home. He would never see her disappointment. Never see that she loved him. It wasn't much, but it was all she had left.

He reached out and grabbed her forearm. "Gina, wait."

She steeled herself and forced a smile that went nowhere near her eyes before saying, "It's over, General. Your honor's safe and your proposal forgotten. Don't worry."

She pulled away and kept walking, back straight, chin lifted. Nick watched her go and for a moment or two was unable to follow her. Once again he felt as though someone had slugged him in the stomach—surprised and a little sick. He couldn't seem to catch his breath, and a deep, throbbing pain had settled in his chest.

As she moved through the crowd, he tried to tell himself he should be counting his blessings. There was no baby. Never had been. Any other man in his position would probably be doing handsprings.

Instead Nick felt as though someone close to him had just died. Stupid, really, he told himself, to be mourning a child that had never existed. And yet, in his mind that baby had been real. A part of Gina and him. A lasting memory of that incredible night.

He'd seen a like pain in her eyes, too, and he knew Gina was feeling the same thing.

The crowd swallowed her. She was lost from sight, and in that moment he knew that if he didn't find her…make her listen…she'd be lost to him forever.

Like the first Marine charging an enemy beachhead, Nick stormed across the floor and pushed his way through the shifting mob of people. As if they sensed he was a man on a mission, those in front of him cleared a path. Those behind muttered complaints. He hardly noticed. Every ounce of his concentration was focused on the search for wavy brown hair and a soft-green dress.

Then he spotted her at the edge of the dance floor, watching the first contestants as they waltzed their way around the perimeter. Coming up behind her, he grabbed her shoulders and turned her to face him.

The music was louder here, and it still couldn't compete with the thudding beat of his own heart.

"We're next," she said calmly, ignoring his firm grip and keeping her gaze carefully averted.

"We're not next for anything until you listen to me."

"There's nothing more to be said," she whispered.

"Wrong, princess," he murmured, and pulled her up close, bending down until they were eye-to-eye and she couldn't avoid looking at him. "I don't want you to forget my proposal," he said.

"The reason for it is gone." The break in her voice echoed the pain in his heart.

"The baby wasn't the reason for it," he muttered thickly, ignoring the interested bystanders. "It was just the excuse I gave myself."

"Whatever," she said, trying to pull free and then surrendering to his strength. Glaring at him, she said, "Will you please let me go?"

He shook his head and scanned her features intently. "I can't, Gina. I never want to let you go. At least, not until I get you to forget about that promise you made and agree to marry me."

She glared briefly at an interested man standing close to them, then looked back at Nick. "The promise isn't part of this anymore."

"It's not?" he asked, and told himself to get the whole story behind that piece of news later.

"No. But that doesn't change anything."

A smattering of applause rose up as the first couple finished their routine. While the judges deliberated, Nick kept talking.

"It changes everything." His voice came low, harsh and desperate. He was fighting for his life, here.

"Nick, you never wanted to get married again, remember? You told me that yourself."

"I changed my mind."

"Why?" she snapped.

"Because I fell in love with you!" he said, his voice loud enough suddenly that several of the nearby women sighed in response.

But the one woman he wanted to respond said nothing. She just stared at him with the brown eyes that would haunt him for the rest of his life. She had to understand. She had to know that everything had changed for him the moment she'd first stepped into his arms at that stupid class.

"Next..." a disembodied voice called over the loudspeaker. "Gina Santini and Nick Paretti, representing the Stanton School of Dance."

"We have to go," Gina said shakily.

"Not yet," he said, gentling his grip on her shoulders, but refusing to release her. "I have to say this."

"Stop. Please."

"Never. I love you, Gina. I'm not afraid to admit that anymore. I love you. I want babies with you."

She blinked, and a solitary tear rolled down her cheek.

Throat tight, Nick kept talking, sensing he was finally near his goal. "I want to wake up every morning for the rest of my life and look into your eyes. I want to argue with you, laugh with you—'' he chuckled shortly ''—*dance* with you. I want it all, Gina, but I can only have it if you say yes.''

''Gina Santini? Nick Paretti?'' the judges called again, more impatiently this time.

She shook her head, but he could see her weakening. Like any good Marine, he pressed his advantage. Pulling her into his arms, he kissed her hard and long, showering her with all the love and want and need rising inside him. And when he let her go, she swayed unsteadily against him.

''Gina?'' he asked, cupping her face with both hands.

''Nick—''

Stubborn woman. Still going to argue.

''Do you love me, Gina?'' he asked,

hoping to God he was right about her feelings for him.

"Of course I love you, but—"

Grinning, Nick shook his head and said, "No buts, princess. Just an answer. Will you marry me?"

A fresh sheen of tears welled up in her eyes, but she nodded, anyway, and said, "Yes, General. I'll marry you."

Applause rose up from their audience, and this time when one of the judges demanded, "Are the Stanton dancers here?" Nick hollered, "Aye-aye, sir!"

Laughing and crying at the same time, Gina slipped her hand into his as he led her out onto the floor. Taking their places for the waltz, Nick whispered, "If we win, you can pick the honeymoon destination. If we lose, I pick."

Gina grinned. "You're gonna love Hawaii, General."

* * * * *

# LARGE PRINT TITLES FOR JULY - DECEMBER 2004

## SILHOUETTE SPECIAL EDITION

| | | |
|---|---|---|
| *July:* | THE BABY LEGACY | Pamela Toth |
| *August:* | THE BRIDE SAID, 'SURPRISE!' | Cathy Gillen Thacker |
| *September:* | WHO'S THAT BABY? | Diana Whitney |
| *October:* | THE VIRGIN BRIDE SAID, 'WOW!' | Cathy Gillen Thacker |
| *November:* | A MAN ALONE | Lindsay McKenna |
| *December:* | MILLIONAIRE'S INSTANT BABY | Allison Leigh |

## SILHOUETTE DESIRE

| | | |
|---|---|---|
| *July:* | THE LAST SANTINI VIRGIN | Maureen Child |
| *August:* | SHEIKH'S WOMAN | Alexandra Sellers |
| *September:* | THE PREGNANT VIRGIN | Anne Eames |
| *October:* | RANCHER'S PROPOSITION | Anne Marie Winston |
| *November:* | TALL, DARK AND WESTERN | Anne Marie Winston |
| *December:* | HER BABY'S FATHER | Katherine Garbera |

## SILHOUETTE SENSATION

| | | |
|---|---|---|
| *July:* | THE WILDES OF WYOMING—ACE | Ruth Langan |
| *August:* | THE UNDERCOVER BRIDE | Kylie Brant |
| *September:* | EGAN CASSIDY'S KID | Beverly Barton |
| *October:* | ROGUE'S REFORM | Marilyn Pappano |
| *November:* | NIGHT OF NO RETURN | Eileen Wilks |
| *December:* | NEVER BEEN KISSED | Linda Turner |

0704-1204 Silh LP